PRAISE FOR

Maggie Sims

"Sexy, witty, emotionally rich writing and incredible **heat** make Maggie Sims a must read! She leaves readers—and her characters—desperate for more! Fierce, fearless heroines are her specialty!"

~ *Tracy Sumner, USA Today Bestselling Author of* The Duchess Society *series*

~*~

"In *Sophia's Schooling*, Maggie Sims strikes a perfect balance of proper manners and delicious perversity. Her characters are deftly sketched, and the flavors of sex and punishment are sure to excite even the most discerning of kinky-historical readers."

~ *Annabel Joseph, NYT and USA Today bestselling author of* The Properly Spanked *series*

~*~

"*Penelope's Passion* is…a wonderful story of forbidden romance from two people in very different life circumstances just trying to do the right thing for both themselves and their families…readers who like an extra spicy historical romance will not want to miss out!"

~ *Golden Angel, USA Today Bestselling Author of the* Bridal Discipline *series*

~*~

"Sims' *Charlotte's Control* is a lovely, steamy read I couldn't put down!"

~ Scarlett Peckham, *USA TODAY Bestselling Author*

Also by Maggie Sims

The School of Enlightenment Series
Roslynn's Rebellion (prequel novella)
Sophia's Schooling (Book 1)
Penelope's Passion (Book 2)
Althea's Awakening (Book 3)
Beth's Behavior (Book 4)

Spin-offs
Helen's House
Ann's Angel (a Christmas short story)

The Control Series
Charlotte's Control
Lyon's Lover
Folly's Folly (2026)

Written as Debbie Charles

Texas Tornadoes Series
Dances with Pucks
Net Pucks and Chill
Spicy as Puck (2026)

Duke's Diversion

by

Maggie Sims

Wayward Dukes Alliance
Book 38

This is a work of fiction. Names, characters, places, and incidents are either the product of the author's imagination or are used fictitiously, and any resemblance to actual persons living or dead, business establishments, events, or locales, is entirely coincidental.

Duke's Diversion

COPYRIGHT © 2025 by Maggie Sims, LLC

All rights reserved. No part of this book may be used or reproduced in any manner whatsoever without written permission of the author except in the case of brief quotations embodied in critical articles or reviews.

No Generative AI Training Use.
For avoidance of doubt, Author reserves all rights, and there are no rights to reproduce and/or otherwise use the Work in any manner for purposes of training artificial intelligence technologies to generate text, including without limitation, technologies that are capable of generating works in the same style or genre as the Work, unless the Author's specific and express permission to do so is given in writing. Nor does anyone have the right to sublicense others to reproduce and/or otherwise use the Work in any manner for purposes of training artificial intelligence technologies to generate text without Author's specific and express permission.

Trade Paperback ISBN 979-8-89044-407-3
Digital ISBN 979-8-89044-408-0
Cover by *Amanda Mariel*

Chapter One

Spring, 1821

Alexander Whitcomb fisted a pillow and crammed it over his head to shut out the repeated knocking. Squinting one eye open, he registered the angle of the sun.

Who was making such a racket so early in the day? And didn't they know he worked at a pub and often drank with his customers? This was the worst part of living upstairs from one's workplace.

Xander's brother Bruce had managed this pub for years and had recently purchased it. Of course, since their mother had married the Earl of Northumberland, who owned it, he got it for a song. Bruce promptly made Xander the closing manager, so he could sleep elsewhere and not be disturbed by early morning deliveries. But none had been scheduled for today, so this infernal banging had to stop.

He let out a sigh into the bedding where he lay diagonally across the too-small bed, facedown. Pushing up, he heaved himself off the bed, ignoring the sawdust in his mouth from that sixth whisky the night before, and scooped up his trousers he'd worn for work to throw on.

Pounding down the stairs barefoot, he shouted, "Hold your knickers, I'm coming."

Opening the door, he blinked in surprise at the stranger standing there. Which, upon reflection, was silly. Any local would have been more respectful of his sleeping hours, as they valued his hostship in the pub. The man was closer to his mother's age than his own, and his black suit was more formal than anyone in Old Shoreston wore, even for church.

"Yes?"

"Mr. Whitcomb?"

"One of 'em," he mumbled.

The stranger frowned. "There is more than one?"

"Long story. Also, not your business." He was not the easiest going at the best of times. Being woken after only five hours of sleep after eight days straight of work and more whisky than normal, he was downright grumpy.

"I'm afraid it may be," the stranger said. Gesturing behind him, he added, "Perhaps I might buy you tea?"

Xander's gaze slid past him to the tea shop diagonally across the road. But then he'd have to trot back upstairs to don shoes, stockings, and a shirt. The stranger was lucky he'd grabbed trousers.

"Nah. You'd better come in." He begrudgingly opened the door wider, closing it and locking it behind them and leading the man through the pub to the small kitchen behind the bar.

"Mr. Jacob Lancaster at your service, Mr. Whitcomb," the man said, sweeping off his hat in a shallow bow. "Solicitor to the Duke of Rutland."

"A duke's solicitor come to Northumberland. And asking for Whitcombs? You sure you don't want the earl or his son, the Lynwoods?" Xander gestured northwest to where his stepfather's stone fortress-slash-home sat on a hill overlooking the wild North Sea.

"Quite."

"I suppose you want tea," Xander grumbled again. At the solicitor's nod, he filled the kettle and set it on the hob. He didn't mean to sound annoyed, but he was.

There was a vague recollection that calling hours began at two in the afternoon in London. Now that was a good rule, as much as he disliked most of London. The city was dirty and far too crowded for his tastes.

He'd spent time down there helping his stepbrother Luke, the younger Lynwood, get Free Your Spirits off the ground. Free Your Spirits was a facility to help men clean themselves up after too much drinking or gambling or whatever other vices Londoners found to waste their lives away. Luke had an unending amount of patience for the spoiled overgrown children of the ton who couldn't manage their lives without liquor. However, Xander did not. They'd been condescending, petulant, and outright rude to him, and he had quickly lost any compassion.

In between moving furniture into rooms, Xander had had to deal with the drunks, many of whom were belligerent. He'd been vomited on, pissed on, punched, and called derogatory names. They waffled between ordering him around like a servant, snubbing him, and begging him to get them just one drink.

After that, Xander was done. He'd gone there as a favor to Luke and his new wife. And their private back garden and plenty of quiet rooms was an oasis in the filth and noise of London. But drunken nobs' attitudes toward hardworking people trying to help them made him want to knock their heads together.

He'd returned to Bruce's establishment, content to manage a pub frequented by working men. Sure, they overindulged and grew surly, but they apologized when they sobered up.

"Would you be willing to indulge me for a moment and explain the multiple Mr. Whitcombs phenomenon, please? I promise I have a good reason."

"'Tain't a secret, so I suppose I could." He shrugged. The man could ask almost anyone in town if he wanted to know badly enough. So as much as he disliked anyone associated with the aristocracy aside from his new family members, Xander answered, "Bruce, my older brother, owns this pub. I work here."

"Er, perhaps you could elaborate a bit more? We only have the record of one son born to James Whitcomb."

Xander retracted his head in shock at Lancaster's use of "we."

Narrowing his gaze, he said, "James, my da, only had one son born—me. He took Bruce in when he married our ma, a year before I came along. Doesn't make him less my brother."

In fact, his parents had chosen Northumberland because the townspeople had been so welcoming. His da set the example by treating both of them equally in both reward and the odd punishment, and the boys were closer than most siblings to this day.

"Ah. Quite right. I understand now, thank you." The man squared his shoulders and reached into his satchel, drawing out some papers. "Well, sir. I have some sad news for you and felicitations, all at once."

Xander wished the kettle would boil quicker. He really needed tea for this.

"Your father's second cousin, John Manners, who was the Duke of Rutland, passed a few months ago. Quite unexpected, as he was not yet forty. The first cousin had died in the war. Neither had produced issue."

"Issue?"

"Children. Heirs."

What a strange way of wording it. Xander noted the man's pursed lips and unblinking gaze. A tendril of dread worked its way up his spine.

"Which," the Londoner paused for emphasis, "makes you the Duke of Rutland, Marquess of—"

"*What?*" The kettle chose that moment to whistle its boil.

Chapter Two

Evie's carriage pulled into the driveway of her aunt's modest home in the town of Rutland, conveniently only a half hour drive from Rutland Manor. That proximity to family had been one of several reasons Evie had been quick to accept the Duke of Rutland's offer of marriage. She'd met him in her first season. Comely enough to catch several suitors' eyes, she'd aimed high. After all, she was the grandniece of a duke and the daughter of an earl.

The carriage was still rocking on its springs when she unlatched the door and sprang from the vehicle without waiting for the step or any assistance.

Aunt Louisa followed her footman out the front door and stood grinning on the steps.

"Aunt Lou!" Evie waved her hands and flew toward her, almost tripping when she neglected to pick up her skirts for the steps. Throwing herself into her aunt's arms, she squeezed the older woman tight. Aunt Louisa was her most beloved family member. She loved her parents to pieces, but they were *parental*. Her aunt was family and friend all wrapped into one, and she'd been excited at the prospect of living within an hour's drive from her.

Her aunt returned the hug and unconsciously echoed Evie's sentiments, whispering in her hair, "Oh my. I could not wish for a better greeting from my favorite niece. How did you fare?"

"It was worth it to see you again." The two days of travel with only her maid for company had been frustrating but imperative to get Aunt Lou's help.

Evie dragged her aunt inside, aiming for the rear parlor. The room doubled as an office and something of a library with a wall of bookshelves, and Louisa detoured to her desk to collect a notebook before sitting across from Evie in a matching armchair.

"Have you seen him?" Evie asked, leaning forward.

"Briefly. He's, mmm, not like the other duke." Her aunt dithered.

"In what way? Is he ugly? Mean?" Alarmed at her own words, Evie gulped. What if he was mean?

John Manners had been the duke named in Evie's marriage contract. When he'd passed unexpectedly, she mourned the loss of a young life but was not overly upset. She had been young and silly when she'd accepted his suit and hadn't realized how much more important common outlooks were than looks and compliments. Instead, she'd relied on unfounded hopes to partner with her future husband to influence the passing of laws to help the poor. Sadly, her betrothed had been a staunch Tory, something she hadn't discovered until after the marriage contract was signed.

Evie had nearly cried when her father told her he'd written to the new duke, some second cousin of the previous one, to renew the betrothal, assuming she was amenable. If only her father hadn't enjoyed his elevation in status from being linked to a duke quite so much. She wished even more he hadn't mentioned it to a few of his peers, causing a risk to her reputation if she or the new duke refused. There was a small amount of wiggle room, but it required finesse to avoid Ton gossip or worse, ostracization.

Whatever that threat, this time around, she planned to do her homework.

Aunt Lou answered her question, "First, I saw him. I did not talk to him. So I cannot speak to his mindset. Second, no, he is not ugly. I meant his physique. He looks like the working-class man he was. Barrel chest, big shoulders, thick arms and thighs…"

Was her aunt *blushing*? Evie giggled and teased, "Auntie! Were you looking at his thighs?"

"All for you, my dear. 'Twas a sacrifice to be sure, but I managed it."

They both snorted before giving in to outright laughter.

Her aunt was the perfect person to help her, and it wasn't due to her proximity to Rutland Manor. Much to her father's regret, the women in her family took what most Ton members would consider an "unnatural" interest in the laws of their country. Her staunchly liberal aunt had influenced her reading and interests, so upon learning of her father's overzealous request on her behalf, Evie had written immediately to Aunt Lou regarding her wish to investigate her new potential husband.

Her aunt had promptly invited her for a visit. However, given the frequency with which past visits had landed them in questionable circumstances, her parents would not have allowed her to go north without a specific reason. So Aunt Louisa had told them that she knew the new duke and would provide an introduction.

Finally, her aunt added, "He is very handsome. Simply in a different way than you might be used to from the Ton set. And I dare say his outlook is rather different as well. He was helping load barrels of wine and ale to go to the manor."

Evie stared, suddenly sober. She needed someone to represent those who performed such jobs, certainly, but a man who was prepared to take on the House of Lords to fix their situation en masse, not help one barrel at a time.

Her aunt murmured, "Have patience, dear. I've been doing some thinking...and some inquiring. All will be well. Apparently, he worked at a pub until now, with no idea he was in line for a dukedom. Perhaps he has not quite found his dukely decorum."

"Oh lordy. Well, that is the purpose of my visit. To find a way to meet him, hopefully more than once, to ascertain that we'll get on well."

Louisa did not really know the new duke; rather, their plan was to devise a way for Evie to learn more about him. After all, she should have a say in marrying a different person than was named in the agreement, a stranger. A betrothal contract should not be treated like a reticule one no longer likes—passed to someone who could get more use out of it.

"That is what I was thinking about before you arrived. I'd heard he is looking to hire two or three new maids."

Evie frowned, unsure where her aunt was going with that statement.

"According to gossip, he had to release a few who were interested in cleaning more than his house, if you take my meaning," her aunt continued.

Evie gasped, shocked at their audacity, although not at her aunt's frankness.

"He gave the first one a generous settlement and letter of reference, so then two others attempted it before he set it as a house rule."

"However did you find this out?" Evie asked.

"Servants talk to other servants. And you know my few are beyond loyal, they are friends." Louisa grinned.

"So, you think to loan him someone of your household?"

Her aunt pursed her lips. "In a manner of speaking…I was thinking you might like to spend some time there…in disguise."

"As a *maid*?" Evie's mouth dropped open. She wasn't above honest work, but she'd never thought of such a possibility. Although it wasn't the worst idea she'd ever heard.

"You know yourself that servants are invisible, especially in a household that size. You'll be able to see what he does each day, who he interacts with, and how those conversations go. What better way to judge his suitability?"

Indeed.

Chapter Three

Xander kept having the same dream. He'd wake up in an enormous manor, with a host of servants ready to bow or curtsy at a moment's notice and a pile of correspondence demanding his attention, with no idea what to do with any of them.

Unfortunately, the dream seemed to last all day. Only at night could he strip off the fine clothes his stepfather, Giles Lynwood, Earl of Northumberland, and better known to most as North, had insisted on buying for him, close his eyes, and remember his simpler life working in his brother's pub.

His mother had been so proud. "I have no doubt that you can manage a dukedom as well as you manage the pub. You deserve this, Xander. I'm excited for you. We'll let you get settled, then come visit. And you must write often."

He was less excited and more overwhelmed, but as she'd pointed out, he'd have help.

The duke's—*his*—solicitor, Jacob Lancaster, had journeyed with him to Rutland, inland and just south of Northumberland, and met with the duke's—*his*—steward, before leaving his direction and assuring Xander that he would respond to any questions or concerns immediately upon receiving them.

Before he'd left Northumberland, Bruce, his stepfather, and his mother had prepared him as best they could.

His mama had told him to befriend the housekeeper. "Have daily or at least weekly check-ins with her, and have a second set of eyes on the books, but unless the house appears derelict, the day-to-day and oversight of the rest of the servants will be handled by her. There will be time later—or hopefully a wife—to manage that."

North had said, "Trust your steward in small increments. Give him the opportunity to prove himself to you or fail. But have Jacob look over the books."

"You think he could be stealing?" Xander was appalled.

"I do not think he is, but neither do I assume he is honest."

"Ugh. What of Jacob?"

"I know Jacob's firm by reputation. And I doubt he would have bothered to come looking for you if he were anything less than loyal. However, the biggest pitfall of inheriting a title is people's expectations. They'll expect you to have money, they'll expect favors and leadership. Indeed, they'll curry attention. Even if you didn't have money, you'd need to worry about who is after your title, particularly the ladies. Jacob says you're flush, so you'll need to consider who is ingratiating themselves looking for that, in addition to the title."

"That sounds bloody awful. I hated London when I was there to work. Now I have a whole extra layer of disgust for it."

"Sadly, you'll likely have to deal with the city and the Ton to some extent in your new role. You hold a seat in the House of Lords now, as well as a London home you should check on periodically. As a Member of Parliament, you have a responsibility to guide the country forward and help govern the people of Britain."

"Geh. I thought having staff was too much responsibility. Is there someone I can pass this along to?"

"Come now," North admonished with a half-smile. "Most men would give their left arm to get a title and a fat purse and retire from working life. It won't be all bad. Plenty of ladies will be interested in entertaining a duke without looking for the title or money. Just be careful of the débutantes."

"And the staff," Bruce added.

"What? Why? Isn't that a lord's privilege?" Xander joked.

North snorted.

His brother frowned and continued. "They work for you. First, Ma would tell you 'tis the height of impropriety to take advantage of that role imbalance. Second, you don't shite where you eat, brother. You should know that after Lisa."

He humphed as North guffawed at his brother's reference to the animosity from a server in the pub after he turned her down for a second night in his bed.

"Fine."

Jacob Lancaster had written to his firm to investigate Munroe, the steward, and send their own evaluation at the earliest possible time. By the time Xander had a handful of new pieces of clothing and three days' lessons done, he was more than ready to leave if only to escape the well-intentioned teachings of his family. His head was going to explode if he had to sit through one more meeting, scribbling notes and hoping his anxiety did not explode out of his chest.

He changed his mind about being ready when they stopped on the circular drive of Rutland Manor, however. The previous duke's parents had both passed, and his sister had married and moved away, so he'd lived in this monstrosity alone when not in London. If Xander's head or anything else exploded, it could take days for anyone to find him in this giant edifice.

Munroe gave him a tour of the place. The gardens alone were as big as the main street of Old Shoreston, where he'd spent the last decade of his life. As for the interior, he had no idea what he was expected to do with eleven guest chambers, several with their own sitting room, and two parlors, not one, a library, and a blooming *ballroom*. He supposed he'd learn. He'd rather not, though; he'd been perfectly content to make the tavern patrons' lives a little better and easier by giving them a pint and a patient ear. Having staff, tenants, and more at other locations relying on him for their bread and butter was more stress than he'd ever looked for. Blazes, after watching his parents struggle to get ahead with two children even before his father's death, he'd never even wooed a girl for fear of accountability.

* * * *

His first full day at Rutland, Xander alternated between meetings with Lancaster and Munroe that made him fear he'd never have adequate knowledge to run the dukedom, much less sit in Parliament. When his heart pounding in his chest moved to a pulse drumming in his temple, he requested a break to walk the gardens.

Munroe had looked confused when Xander asked the second time, and the London solicitor leaned in to say, "You're the duke. We are here at your convenience, Your Grace."

Apparently, politeness was not valued in dukes. He

rolled his eyes again.

He'd asked what time supper would be served and got another strange expression from the housekeeper before she blinked and said, "Whatever time you'd like, Your Grace."

The one bright spot in his new circumstances was his bed. The giant cherry wood bed frame with fancy carved posts in his fancy ducal bedroom was the first one large enough for his build. Between its size and the extravagant bedding, he slept better than he ever had. Although that might be from exhaustion. Managing a pub had been physically challenging, but the mental toll of his new world drained him in a different way.

After a few days of transition, Lancaster excused himself back to London, informing Xander that he was in capable hands with Munroe, and he was only a letter away.

Xander took another sennight to find a routine that worked for him. Irritation with all the demands waiting for him was slower, and he was less likely to take that out on Munroe if he used the mornings to read alone at the duke's—*his*—massive desk in the library, allowing himself to feel overwhelmed when needed and to consolidate his questions. Munroe would join him in the afternoon, and they'd move to the small table and chairs by a window, where they'd work through whatever the next element of the dukedom Munroe thought he needed to learn that day.

This morning, he re-entered the library and plopped down in his chair. The desk faced the door with his back to the glass veranda doors so he turned to stare outside at the rolling fields. That view was more compelling than bookshelves and the hall door; he could not fathom why anyone would have placed the desk facing away from it.

Frustrated, he turned to start work. *Wait a minute*. He was a duke now. Stepping out into the hall, he called to the footman by the front door. "Hullo. I'm sorry, I have forgotten your name."

"Ferguson, sir. How may I assist?" The man trotted over, bowing his head.

"No, your first name."

The man's eyes went wide. He swallowed and answered, "Duncan, sir."

"Duncan, would you be so kind as to help me move the desk, please?" Xander wasn't sure he'd ever rid himself of asking people when he wanted help or service. He didn't care if other nobs expected it like their due, he'd never be like them.

"Of course." The man stepped into the library. "Ah, let me call for another servant, sir."

"Why?"

"I shan't be able to move that alone without scraping the floors, and then Mrs. Betters will have my head."

"Duncan," Xander said on a sigh, trying to find his patience. "I am an able-bodied man who was lifting casks half his days until a fortnight ago. I will lift the other side."

Duncan opened his mouth to argue, but closed it.

Xander almost laughed, suspecting the man was debating between arguing that a duke shouldn't do that sort of thing and arguing with a duke, period. To expedite the solution, he moved to one end of the table and gestured. "I want to rotate it a quarter turn, so I have the outdoors on one side and the interior door on the other, with the rest of the room and the fire in front of me."

"Of course, sir." Duncan grabbed a few books off the

shelf nearest him and placed them on the piles of documents on the desk so they wouldn't spill.

"Ah, good thought. Thank you."

The footman blinked before saying, "Certainly, Your Grace."

After they'd adjusted the desk and Xander brought the chair around, he sat to test it, looking in both directions. "So much better, don't you think?"

Duncan blinked twice and took a moment to form his reply. "Definitely, Your Grace. You can enjoy the outdoors whilst keeping an eye on anyone who might think to disturb you."

Xander barked a short laugh. "Well put, Duncan. 'Ta."

The footman re-shelved the books before heading back to his post in the hall.

Alone again but in a better mood, Xander tackled the rather daunting amount of correspondence awaiting him. Munroe had opened the letters in case anything urgent required dukedom funds or arbitration. He'd been kind enough to separate letters into two piles. One was composed of letters of condolences and felicitations, often on the same page, regarding the previous duke's passing and his ascension. Xander planned to ignore those as long as possible.

The second pile was more time-sensitive notes, including House of Lords business to review.

Xander picked up a page from the top of the pile.

To Alexander Whitcomb, Third Duke of Rutland,

He doubted he'd ever get comfortable seeing that in writing or hearing himself introduced as such. And the "Your Graces" were downright annoying. He kept looking around for a chit named Grace. He continued reading, phrases leaping out at him.

...part of an alliance...here to help...visit in the coming weeks...

He straightened in his desk chair. There was an alliance by dukes, to help dukes? He leaned back. Of course there was. Perhaps there could be an alliance of dockworkers to help each other, too, and tavern workers, and whatever else. But none of them had the time or the wherewithal to form such a thing. Even if they did, it would only take the coffers of one wealthy merchant, earl, or dare he say it, duke, to smite them. An alliance, however, would keep power centered exactly where dukes wanted it—among themselves.

Throwing the letter aside, he moved to the next one and spent the better part of an hour trying to decipher the references and the attached proposed bill from the House of Commons. That, too, was tossed to the side. Sighing with frustration, he thunked his elbows on the desk and threaded his fingers through his hair to support his head. Staring down at the desk, he closed his eyes in frustration. He read the newspapers, of course. However, the governance of the country was so far removed from everyday life for most Brits that none of them could speak to the pros and cons of a law or even whether it benefited them directly. Half the documents revised or amended older laws, which meant he'd need to see if archives were kept at this house by the former dukes or request them from London. It was exhausting.

A rustle from behind his left brought his head up and around. He hadn't heard anyone come into the office. A maid in a frilled mob cap stood nearby.

Munroe always knocked. The whole point of working alone in the mornings was for these private anxiety attacks.

Now, however, someone had witnessed his silent panic. He narrowed his gaze at her, channeling his newfound ducal energy.

She nodded to him, appearing immune. "They're expanding the Insolvent Debtors Act to Ireland, hmm?"

"I beg your pardon?" Was this part of maids' training for a duke's household? He was relatively sure she was one of the newer hires, and that the two maids who had made sexual advances toward him would not have had that observation even if they'd spent an hour with the letter as he had.

"The bill." She tilted her head to the second letter he'd thrown aside. "I hadn't considered Ireland. Rather myopic of me, wasn't it? I'm glad they are rectifying it."

He gaped. Half aware that he resembled a fish, opening and closing his mouth without emitting any words, he had a crazy thought. If he hadn't been sure before, he was now. This had to be a dream becoming a nightmare because a lovely chit he'd never hesitate to tup before was suddenly off limits. Worse, the minute she opened her mouth, she proved she knew more about the governing of the country than he did.

Chapter Four

Realizing what she'd just done, Evie caught her breath, aghast. Servants didn't comment on Parliamentary matters. Hellfire, not all of them knew how to read.

She'd spent her first few days cleaning whatever below-stairs rooms the duke was not using, gathering her bravery to venture into the library and thinking up ways to interact other than spilling something on him. She'd groaned when she'd seen the thirty-person set of silverware to be polished in the dining room. Then again at the mount of wood in the library to be dusted and polished. Bookshelves, windowsills, tables—a round one for a light meal, the low one in the seating area, and a side table, and the duke's desk.

She was behind the breakfast table on her knees, half dusting, half skimming the titles on the shelves in the far corner when the duke entered the library. Her heart raced as she remained quiet. This was the chance she'd been waiting for, to observe him without appearing impertinent.

He was quickly engrossed, staring so hard at the papers before him she thought they might ignite.

She edged closer to get a better look at him. His fingers fidgeted with a pen seemingly held to take notes, and his brow was furrowed. Despite those signs of irritation, he was as overwhelming and rugged as her aunt had said. And goodness, that man was thick in all the best ways, no skinny fop in heeled shoes and floral waistcoat. He wasn't even wearing a waistcoat and in the few glimpses she'd had of him coming and going, she had yet to see him in a cravat.

She wanted to smooth away his frown, run her fingers through his thick blond-brown hair, and help him. Her father only looked like that when he was reading some horribly oppressive bill. Curious, she glanced over his shoulder. Seeing the expansion of the Insolvent Debtors Act, a burst of fear shook her. Did he hate this, a law that she greatly admired?

She must have made some noise, because his head snapped up and he glared. This close, his dark piercing eyes stared as though he saw right through her pretense—indeed straight through her clothing. Without a cravat, she caught a tantalizing peek of neck and chest hair through his open shirt collar.

Her thoughts scattered at the view, and she spoke without thinking. Flutters in her belly distracted her from his open-mouthed reaction to her comments. Lingering to decipher his expression was out of the realm of possibility.

Instead, she fled to the kitchen to find the housekeeper. "Mrs. Betters, the duke seemed, er, agitated. I wonder if it might be best if I work in the front parlor today and finish the library another time?" Everyone wanted to make a good impression on the new duke, and she knew she was taking shameless advantage of that with her excuse.

She'd never spent much time with her parents' housekeepers, but Harriet Betters was hardworking, fair, and intelligent. In fact, Mrs. Betters' discerning gaze had already made Evie wonder if the woman suspected her deception. Her aunt had recommended her, and her servants had given Evie a quick tutorial on dusting, polishing, and rug beating. She was young enough that she could claim only one household as her experience, giving her leeway to ask "how things were done here." But she couldn't disguise her accent, which was very much not working class. When Mrs. Betters asked during their first meeting, she'd waved a hand and cited an earl's London household as the reason. The housekeeper had dropped the subject and hired her, but watched Evie closely.

By now, the housekeeper had seen her willingness to work and relaxed, smiling at Evie when she came with questions. She said, "That'll be fine. Be sure to get back to the library tomorrow, assuming His Grace is in better spirits. Remember, the goal is to be inconspicuous."

She gulped. Discussing a Parliamentary bill with him after reading over his shoulder was not conducive to invisibility. She must do better.

She stayed out of sight the rest of the day, hoping he'd forget the whole thing. Only in her narrow servant's bed did she consider his appeal as a future husband. Just as her aunt had warned her, he was rather undukelike in many ways. But on that physique, she could live without formal clothing when they were at home. She'd never realized the hollow at the base of a man's neck could be so alluring, like it was made for her fingertip…or her tongue.

She dreamed of his throat, finding it so fascinating that when she woke she worried she'd never look him in the eye again. However, her greater concern was being more careful in what she said.

The next day, she started her dusting duties near the duke's desk before he arrived, then quickly moved to the other end of the library when he entered the room. Once he settled, she spent as much time sneaking sidelong glances at him as she did dusting.

His face was too rugged and masculine to be beautiful, but she could stare at it for hours. Each facet reflected his life to date, especially his eyes. Umber-colored, they contained a mix of warmth and directness, inviting one to meet him as an equal. She imagined he sold a lot of drinks in that pub he'd managed with those eyes and a smile. His time outside—no carriages for him—was reflected in his tanned skin, and smile lines spoke to a lifetime of joy, although she'd not seen him smile since she arrived. Unlike the fashion of the day, he kept his hair short enough that only a hint of the wave highlighted the lighter streaks, as though he was short on time to style it. All in all, it was a breathtaking visage even before she got to the exposed wedge of throat and the rest of him.

On the second morning, she was able to catch a glimpse of the papers he'd left scattered. There was a pile to one side, facing down, and the page left up began in the middle of a sentence. That likely meant he had become so frustrated with perusing it the day before, he'd left it mid-read. Sure enough, an hour and a half later, he was muttering under his breath and raking his hand through his hair. The library had so much to dust that she had plenty of time to observe him, and she watched him covertly. As much as she enjoyed his masculine physique, he appeared so frustrated that she spent more time wishing she could help him without giving herself away.

The next day, he'd been there less than an hour when he cleared his throat loudly, making her jump. Swallowing her squeak of surprise, Evie cast yet another furtive look. Goodness, he seemed to be staring at her—her backside, to be specific. She stared blindly at the books in front of her on the shelf, dusting slowed to lackadaisical swipes. It was one thing to be attracted to a man she might marry, but quite another for a duke to hungrily eye someone he thought was a servant.

A small part of her wished she knew enough about him to decide whether she wanted the betrothal contract, so she could explore the promise of pleasure, society rules be damned. Another part was ready to cast aside those rules and her maid's dress at his command. However, she had her reputation and future to think of. Stepping back, she nodded at the shelves as though satisfied with their condition, and then sped out of the room to find another place to dust.

Chapter Five

Xander watched the pretty maid flee the room yet again. She'd caught him staring at her arse, despite his family's lectures and needing to dismiss maids for similar acts.

She was a puzzle with her knowledge of the aristocracy and audacious manners, and that intrigued him as much as her pert figure. Mrs. Betters would know more. However, he needed to find a balance between learning about the young woman who occupied far too much of his thoughts and showing inappropriate interest in any servant.

Heading toward the kitchen, he paused in the doorway to look for the housekeeper.

All activity came to an abrupt halt at his appearance. Xander closed his eyes and gave a minute head shake. He couldn't even look for the person he wanted to speak to without upsetting some balance no one had taught him.

"I'm looking for Mrs. Betters," he said. His voice was closer to a growl than he would have liked due to his frustration, and he cleared his throat. "Perhaps someone could send her to the library? Sorry to disturb."

Withdrawing, he returned to the library but hadn't yet rounded his desk when the housekeeper trotted into the room. "You wished to see me, Your Grace?"

"Yes. I looked for you in the kitchen, which seemed

to upset the staff. Was I supposed to do something else?"

"Your Grace, of course you're welcome to visit the kitchen any time you'd like. 'Tis your kitchen, after all—"

Xander cut her off with a slashing motion. "Yes, yes. My kitchen, my everything. However, I dislike disturbing people and hate feeling like I've done something wrong if there is a more comfortable path for everyone." He gulped. "And I'm sorry to have cut you off. I'm annoyed at my ignorance, not anyone else."

She blinked at his apology, took a moment, then said, "Please do not fash yourself, my lord."

His brows rose at the less formal address but she didn't notice, for which he was grateful. He'd ask her to call him that in the future after they cleared this up.

She continued, "We are here to help; indeed, we're happy to do so. Habits are easy to fall into, but I'll inform the staff again that there may be new ways of doing things with a new duke in residence."

"Thank you, Mrs. Betters. I'm still curious, however. What would the previous duke have done?"

"He'd likely have asked one of the footmen to find me and bring me to you."

"Ah." He looked around and muttered, "Blazes, I need never leave this chair, eh? Ridiculous to send hardworking people running around when I am perfectly capable."

The housekeeper almost snorted, managing to keep it to an audible exhale through her nose.

He glanced back.

A smile teased her lips. She made a small curtsy. "If I may, Your Grace, you have much to accomplish here, and more to worry about than this household. We are here to support you in that endeavor, in whatever way you may wish."

He'd frowned at the formal title again, but understood her point. His time was valuable to managing a much larger staff than the ones there in Rutland.

"I'm accustomed to much more movement in my previous role, but I suppose I can contain that to outdoors." He sighed. "However, I'd appreciate you reminding the staff that not only is there a new duke, but he's much less formal, so if I appear in an unlikely place, it is not because I'm checking on them, or need someone to run in response to a summons, or anything else. Indeed, it may well be because I'm lost in this monstrous house."

A giggle erupted from Mrs. Betters, and she slapped her hand over her mouth, appalled. Her eyes went wide over her hand, and she pulled it away to start, "Your Grace, I apol—"

"No, please. You can laugh if I say something funny. And no more 'Your Grace.' 'My lord' will do if you must. I was Xander to my staff in the past."

She nodded once and asked, "Now, how may I be of assistance, my lord?"

He smiled at her easy acceptance of his preference. "I'd like to get a list of all the servants' names, a short note regarding their duties, and how long they've been here."

"Certainly. I'll have that to you later today. Is there something in particular I can help you with? Maybe a specific concern?"

He wondered if she'd have asked his predecessor that, but he couldn't fault her for asking after he'd just invited informality. His guilty conscience probably had prompted that question, anyway. "Not at all. 'Tis yet another aspect of this new world I need to learn. I should learn people's names if I'm going to ask them to run my errands, don't you think?"

She grinned. "That would be lovely. Thank you, my lord."

As she departed, Xander sat back and propped his elbows on the arm of his chair, steepling his fingers. The first step of assuaging his curiosity about the impertinent maid had been made. Perhaps he could track mud into the library to force her to work in his presence. Even better, maybe he could leave paperwork on the table in the far corner and then pepper her with questions if he caught her reading it. Most of all, he was dying to see the color of her hair, hidden under that mobcap she wore, and the shape of her body obscured by the drab shapeless uniform.

He stared into space, picturing a much different maid's uniform. Perhaps only a shift. Or a shift and a corset so whenever she leaned over…

North's warning sounded in his head, and he jerked upright, swearing at himself. He'd never do such a thing, but he shouldn't even be entertaining thoughts of the pretty servant. He needed to find a way to take the edge off other than his hand, but out here in the country, options were limited. No, even with all the options in the world, that woman's combination of audacity, intelligence, and a delectable figure would intrigue him. If only she were within reach morally as much as she was physically.

Scrubbing a hand through his hair again, he returned to the drudgery of learning and opining on the country's laws.

Chapter Six

At the servants' supper in the kitchen, Evie heard about the duke's appearance and his search for Mrs. Betters. Everyone at the long table was speculating about his reason.

When Harriet entered, the table grew quiet. Standing at the end of the table, she stated matter-of-factly, "I expect you're all eager to know what his lordship wanted. First, I'd like to remind you what I said after the news of the old duke. Every nob has their own way of doing things. His Grace reinforced that, noting that his are liable to be less formal than others we've worked for, due to his circumstances. So if you see him in unexpected places or doing unexpected things, do not worry. Simply do as you always have—ask how you can be of assistance or go about your business."

She made eye contact with everyone at the table, waiting for a nod of acknowledgement from each person before moving on. Evie agreed eagerly. This gave her a bit more leeway if she slipped up again in respecting the line between servant and lord.

Harriet continued, "Now, as to what he was looking for, 'twas a list of all everyone he employs in this household—"

A buzz started at the table. Every staff member had been nervous about his perspective on their duties and performance.

The housekeeper held up a hand. "Calm down. I asked him the purpose of such a request, and he indicated it is so that he can learn the names of the people who work for him. No one should be concerned at this time. He seems very genuine, approachable even."

Hmm. Evie would like to approach him, from the front or the back, and climb him like the tree trunk he resembled. When the dinner rolls passed across her, she returned to the present and grabbed one, checking her chin for drool. But of course there was no need to worry, as Cook would take it as a compliment.

The next day, having finished the dusting of her assigned rooms, she was due to start polishing furniture. Once again, she began in the front parlor, the memory of his gaze on her arse fresh. When a troupe of horses sounded on the circular drive, she peered around the curtains. Outriders preceded a carriage which stopped in front of the steps to the large double doors.

Her eyes widened at the crest of the Duke of Cranbrook. There had been no talk of any visitors, much less a duke. Or her great uncle.

She should warn Harriet. But she paused to watch the step being placed after the carriage door opened. The Duke of Cranbrook exited to reveal a second passenger. She gasped when his son, her second cousin, the Marquess of Hollibrook, alighted. Oh my, two dukes and a marquess under a single roof. Back in London, that would be an enormous coup. Ton gossip would thrive for days on just what they might be discussing. Particularly if two of them were family and one was her betrothed. But alas, she was a maid for the moment.

She peered closer at the men and estimated it had been at least eight years since she'd seen her relatives.

They'd visited Cranbrook, which meant she'd been around twelve, gangly legged and flat-chested. Hopefully, neither would recognize her after that much time, but her best bet was to stay out of sight. She could not afford to have her identity exposed; she hadn't yet had the chance to learn anything beyond the duke's looks and apparent disdain for neckcloths and jackets. Besides, her reputation would be in shreds if anyone knew she'd been sleeping in a single man's house without a chaperone, no matter what her supposed role was.

She rushed out of the parlor, warned the footman by the door, then trotted straight back to the kitchen.

The housekeeper emerged as she neared. Skidding to a stop, Evie heaved a breath and gushed, "The Duke of Cranbrook and the Marquess of Hollibrook are outside. Did no one know of their visit?"

"What?" Harriet whisper-yelled.

"They would never visit without either an invitation or an appropriate notice of their call. Does His Grace not know he needs to warn the household to prepare? Hellfire, what if Cook doesn't have enough food for an appropriate dinner?" Evie shook her head, agog at the temerity of their employer.

Harriet's eyes went wide, and she was slow to respond as her gaze slipped to something behind Evie.

She turned, following the housekeeper's line of sight and gulped. The wayward duke in question stood there staring at her with an arched brow. Frustration fought with embarrassment. Only this duke would follow her to the back hall. Although in fairness, he'd probably seen her run by the library door. Her face grew hot as she said, "I beg your pardon, Your Grace. I only meant— Someone of your background— Never mind. You have my apology. We are here to serve you and your guests at your pleasure."

Now both his brows neared his hairline as he smirked at her. He rumbled in that baritone which never failed to send a shiver down her spine, "How did you know who they were?"

"I spied the crest on the carriage out the front parlor window," she replied, ignoring the strange look from the housekeeper.

But she could not avoid his next question, which likely mirrored the housekeeper's confusion. "And you recognize ducal crests?"

"Oh! Uh, some? From the last household I was in," she fumbled with yet another error. She'd been worried she wouldn't know how to properly bang rugs out or spill spirits when refilling decanters but never thought her knowledge of the Ton would give her away.

The housekeeper asked, "You said there were two?"

"Yes," Evie answered with a firm nod.

Harriet turned to her. "Go tell Cook. I'll have the upstairs staff prepare two guest suites."

"Mrs. Betters," the duke's voice stopped the housekeeper in her tracks, and Evie slowed her trot to a crawl to hear what he'd say next. "You and the staff have my apologies for not informing you of my guests. I did not pay attention to the date in their letter. I'm sure your best efforts will be excellent."

Evie gaped. A duke had apologized to a servant. What would come next? Flying elephants? Him giving them a raise? Maybe even asking for lessons in dukeishness—or was it ducality? She giggled all the way to tell Cook about their honored guests, despite the chef's fearsome temper.

Chapter Seven

That outrageous maid had again witnessed his shame; in fact, she'd come near to upbraiding him for it. Xander shook his head. The housekeeper had blinked several times at his apology before murmuring, "Quite all right, Your Grace. If you'll excuse me."

Despite his embarrassment, when she'd turned for the stairs, he'd spun to watch the receding and lovely backside of the cheeky maid. A vision rose of him calling her in front of him to reprimand her and offering some creative ways as penance for chastising him.

His cock stirred in his trousers, and he reluctantly turned away. He had two nobs to deal with. The thought was enough to wither even the most enthusiastic cockstand.

Two hours later, his head was spinning again. The duke and marquess had invited Munroe to join them and had offered to point out where the greatest risks of charlatans and swindlers, both male and female, might be. With his acceptance, they'd systematically gone through an overview of his holdings—estates, investments, and staff. Well, not servants such as the maid with the heart-shaped bouncy bottom, but solicitors, secretaries, and stewards.

They'd helped him further prioritize what to learn and address, praising Munroe for his efforts.

When they turned to the pitfalls of being a duke,

Xander raised a hand to stop them. "First, I've already gotten this lecture from my stepfather."

The Duke of Cranbrook chuckled, nodding, as he'd mentioned to Xander that he had a passing acquaintance with North.

"I've already had to release three members of my staff due to inappropriate behavior. Also, if I hear any more things to worry about, I might walk out. And, no offense intended"—he gulped a breath—"but whilst I hate most of my new duties, no duke should be allowed to complain about his lot in life. I should know, I've seen the other side."

He wasn't sure he could hold himself to that, but he'd made his point. Both of the older men dipped their heads in acknowledgement.

The Duke of Cranbrook said, "Understood. However, just in case you should encounter trouble, we have created a support group of sorts. The Wayward Dukes Alliance. To that end, there remains one last order of business."

The younger man produced a signet ring. An emblem was set behind a dark red stone.

When it was proffered, Xander took it. Peering, he thought he saw an elaborate "WD."

He tried to hand it back, but both men shook their heads. The Duke of Cranbrook said, "All members wear this or have it. If you see someone with it on, you know they will help you in any way they can. If you need help yourself but cannot get to one of us in person, send the ring and we'll know 'tis urgent. Try it on."

Xander attempted to slide it on to his fourth finger, but it did not make it to the second knuckle. It fit onto his fifth, but there was no way he was wearing a ring there.

He'd be afraid to lose the thing. And that finger was for fops and dandies, far too pretentious for him. Of course, a duke's ring would be designed for slimmer hands than his. They'd never had to haul kegs, shovel snow, or any other of the myriad tasks which had been his life.

He passed it back, not sure how to word his reluctance.

He needn't bother. Hollibrook produced another ring, identical to the first except in circumference. That one was a tight fit, but he shoved it onto his fourth finger, willing to force it in order to pacify these new allies. As it slid home, he grunted and muttered, "There."

"Excellent. Why don't we enjoy the evening? We shall check in with you before we depart tomorrow."

Munroe chimed in, "You're leaving tomorrow?"

Catching his alarmed glance at his steward, the Duke of Cranbrook chuckled and explained. "When people travel for multiple days to reach a destination, they prefer to enjoy their visit for a few days. However, we suspected you'd be overwhelmed, and as I said in the letter, we came because we live close—only a few hours ride."

Xander nodded and caught a movement at the door. The pretty maid—his curiosity about the color of her hair under her mobcap had only increased—was gesturing at him. He frowned.

She mimed pouring a drink in a glass then bringing it to her mouth.

Ohh. This whole drinking during the day thing was a nobs' benefit he could get behind. If he could only remember it. She seemed to know things the other servants did not. Or perhaps they all knew protocols but only she dared point his failings out. Regardless, he didn't care as long as her wisdom could benefit him.

He inclined his head and turned to his guests. "Shall we adjourn to the parlor and have a drink before supper, then?"

Their smiles told him she'd saved him from embarrassment. Well, that was a pleasant change from her discovering it. Perhaps he ought to ask her for lessons.

* * * *

After a surprisingly relaxed supper, there were more drinks and cigars—for the two older men, anyway—in the parlor.

Xander had been relieved to see a veritable feast laid out, with several options of grilled fish and meats, and four courses. He hoped the servants hadn't ended up with bread and cheese as a result and made a mental note to talk to Cook on the morrow.

Another impressive buffet was set out for breakfast, and his visitors rose earlier than he'd expected, based on his limited knowledge of aristocrats and London hours. Country hours must be different even for entitled—*er, titled*—lords. He was still on tavern hours, but he'd instructed his valet to wake him at the first sign of his visitors stirring.

The poor man almost skipped in eagerness. To date, Xander had barred him from his room other than to coordinate baths and collect his laundry. Given the valet's reaction, he surmised Frazer must be nervous for his job and decided to review staffing soon and reassure servants wherever possible.

This morning, he needed Frazer's help knotting a cravat without strangling himself. North had helped him for the journey here, and he hadn't bothered with one in the house. But needs must for guests.

After breakfast, he made all the appropriate noises as Cranbrook and Hollibrook donned their outerwear.

"Your Grace, Lord Hollibrook, I very much appreciate your assistance and guidance. I have more work to do to learn everything I need, but I look forward to seeing you again." He actually meant that, too, much to his surprise. Even so, the back of their carriage was still visible through the front window as he stood in the main hall and tugged at the neckcloth.

"There's a pin, Your Grace," the pretty maid murmured to him, trailing her duster along a side table.

He looked around for a mirror, his hands still clenched in the folds of white linen.

"Shall I help?"

His brows rose. Any other servant would ask timidly. She suggested it, as bold as could be. Frankly, it was a refreshing change. And what could it hurt? He'd already surmised she could help him with a good many aspects of this new life, filling in the gaps that Munroe could not.

"Please." His tone was gruff as he dropped his hands and raised his chin to get out of her way.

She sidled closer, tilting her head to peer at the mess he'd made.

"Hold this." She held out the feather duster.

He took it without thinking, then caught the footman's owlish look. His eyes were so wide that Xander pictured them possibly rolling out of his face. A quiet snort escaped him.

"My lo—Your Grace?" The maid turned her doe eyes, dark brown and huge in her face, up to meet his.

He whispered, barely moving his lips, although why

he was concerned about embarrassing her, he didn't know, "The footman yon seems very concerned that I am holding your duster."

Her gaze slid to the side. Glancing back at him, she snorted, too. "My apologies, Your Grace. It seemed the most expedient way to stop you from strangling yourself."

Impudent wench. He fell a degree more in lust with her at that moment, gazing down at her ivory skin, full lips in the palest of pinks, and delicately arched brows. In his old life, he'd kiss the impudence right out of her, then find a quiet corner in which to tup her—a desk, bar, keg of ale, whatever was at hand.

His cock woke and stretched. Taking a deep breath, he willed his body back to sleep.

"There," she said with a firm nod. His cravat slid around the back of his neck and he tore his gaze away from her face. Ah, she held his cravat pin—who knew?—in one hand and was tugging the cloth off him with the other. Presenting them to him with a flourish, hands held high, she grinned and said, "Shall we trade?"

"What? Oh," he said, confused until he remembered the duster in his hand. Returning it to her, he asked, "May I have a word with you in my office?"

She leaned in and said in a low tone, "You don't need to ask, Your Grace. I am at your command."

He swallowed. His cock was not going to take that image lying down. Turning away from her quickly, he walked to the stair banister first, draping the cravat over it and securing the pin in one end, before gesturing, "Come, then."

Gulping again at his poor choice of wording, he moved into his office to hover behind his desk, where the worst of his sins would be hidden. Gesturing her to a chair, he sat. "Tea?"

She laughed at him. Mouth open, no quiet titter, she full out cackled.

"I have always been courteous to my employees—" he twisted his mouth, recalling one or two laggards—and Lisa if he was honest—who would not agree. "—and see no reason to stop now."

She blinked. "I beg your pardon, my lord, that was not well done of me." Shrugging a shoulder, she added, "Why not?"

After moving to the door to request a tea tray with biscuits, he returned to his desk. Her laughter had at least cured his need to hide. Now he got right to the point. "You seem remarkably well-versed in etiquette for a maid."

She clenched and unclenched her hands in her lap. "I told you—a London household…"

"Yes, well. I see no reason to ignore it. I'd like you to help me…" He still didn't know her name. "Uh, Miss—? What is your name, please?"

"Al—Mullens. Evie Mullens," she said, looking more nervous than before.

"Miss Mullens. Perhaps I could borrow you from your other duties for an hour or two a day?"

She bit her lip, one corner of her mouth tilting up.

Realizing his error, he tried for a firmer tone. "Perhaps I shall borrow you from your duties. When I need you."

She nodded then winked. "Certainly, Your Grace. And better."

Blazes. How was he going to avoid a cockstand during meetings with her? She was exactly the type of saucy wench he'd always pursued for bedsport. With the ugly maid uniform obscuring her features, he could ignore the attraction if it were only physical. But her sauciness and wit lured him to quiet her mouth with his own. And now he'd gone and set them up to spend hours together in solitude every day.

* * * *

The dinner with the dukes had been surprisingly less taxing and more comfortable than Xander had anticipated, and he was not yet ready to return to solitary suppers. However, he had not yet convinced Munroe to join him for his evening repast, and after having company, the dining room felt particularly empty.

The village had a pub though, and he was far more comfortable with that fare than the fancy meals the ducal kitchen prepared. With a grimace, he recalled Miss Mullen's agitation about informing the staff of changes and told the footman he'd be dining in the village when he requested his coat.

The man blinked, the strongest reaction Xander had gotten from him, so he surmised the village would be a tad surprised as well. Glancing down at himself, he recalled his stepfather's lecture about presenting himself properly and turned to the stairs, calling for his valet.

Frazer was panting as he met Xander at his bedroom door and looked far more excited than the circumstances called for.

"I need one of those infernal cravats, Frazer. And, I dunno, a waistcoat and jacket, I suppose. What does a duke wear to a public house?"

"A pub—" Frazer swallowed the rest of his exclamation. "Your Grace, would you like me to arrange for a private room there?"

"What? Why? God sakes, man, if I wanted to eat alone, I could do that here."

The valet gulped as he tied Xander's neckcloth. "Surely you don't mean to eat—"

"—with the riffraff?" He narrowed his gaze at the servant. "Careful. I was one of the riffraff a few months ago."

"Your Grace, I'd never have said that."

When Frazer looked uncomfortable but did not finish his sentence, Xander lifted his chin and said, "Tell me."

"'Tis just that the village folks might react a bit funny to having a duke in their midst. They go there to relax, but as they don't know you like we do here at the house, they will be on their best behavior for you."

"Hang it, I cannot even enjoy a good pub meal and an ale without others feeling the need to bow and scrape?" Xander's hands went to his cravat to rip his valet's hard work apart.

"If I may, Your Grace." Frazer's hands hovered over his, not quite daring to physically stop him. "There is only one way to get past this. Go, and keep going, until it becomes the norm for them. Maybe stay off in a corner and don't watch folks. If you leave them alone, they'll leave you alone and become accustomed to you—"

"—lurking." Xander laughed. "I like the way you think, Frazer. You have my gratitude. I shall try it."

He rode his favorite horse, a gelding that was easy and calm, as he had walked more than rode in his previous life. But he could not see dragging out the stablehands and the carriage driver as well as the vehicle itself for the few miles to town, and he didn't know the area well enough to walk. Cranbrook and Hollibrook had also warned him to be more careful now, as a duke's purse or even a duke himself were targets for bandits.

As he pulled up to the public house, an idea formed. Handing his mount to the stablehand, he ducked around the back of the building to the kitchen door where deliveries were sent.

There, he knocked. A red-faced cook opened it, took one look at him, and said with a head toss, "Wrong door, gov'nor. Go 'round front wid ya."

"I need to speak to the manager, please."

"Oh, ya do, do ya?" The man's tone became mocking. "Who shall I say is calling?"

"Xander Whitcomb."

The cook blinked. "The *duke*? Oi, come in, Your Grace. Unless you'd rather wait there?" He made an aborted attempt at a bow, then gestured, clearly at a loss. "'Tis rather warm in here."

"I don't wish to interrupt any more than I have."

"'Tis no matter. Hang on a second." The man turned and bellowed as he held the door for Xander to step in. "Banks, get your arse back here. The *duke* is asking for ya."

Xander sighed. So much for staying out of the public eye to allow villagers some peace.

The kitchen noise stopped. No pots banged, knives chopped, voices called to each other. The staff were statues, faces turned to him.

He gave a single nod. "Evening."

"Evening, sir."

"Please, don't mind me. I used to work in a place like this, as I'm sure you've heard."

They nodded, still nonplussed, until the manager came banging through the door from the front. "What are you yelling about, Fletcher?"

Following him were two serving girls, asking about food orders. The two cooks and the dishwasher went back to their tasks, albeit with more subdued movements.

"Sir." Fletcher had lost his words and gestured between Xander and the manager several times.

"Xander Whitcomb." Xander nodded. "I recently moved here. I wonder if I might borrow you for a few minutes. I can wait if it is busy out there."

"Your Grace. I am honored. Please, why are you back here? I have a private room available for you," Banks said, wringing his hands.

Xander waved a hand in a circular motion, trying to entice the man to step into the alley.

His brows pinched in confusion, he followed Xander and closed the door on the curious looks.

"What is your name, my good man?"

"Oliver Banks. Most call me Banks."

"Well, Banks, as I was telling your staff in there, until recently, I worked in a pub like this one, for my brother. So, I have a proposition for you."

The man's brows rose.

"I am quite sure the town knows my story. To elaborate, I'd be far more comfortable doing what you're doing and wearing what you're wearing than I am in this costume." He waved a hand down himself.

Banks smiled. "Yes, I suppose I can see that."

"I'm not complaining, mind you. I know I should count my blessings, and I do. However, the transition is…perhaps not painful, but tedious. Onerous. Once in a while, I want nothing more than to carry a few kegs, pour a few drinks, and eat a nice simple pub meal." He leaned in. "Please don't tell my chef that, she works very hard."

The manager grinned and nodded at his last words. "How can I help, Your Grace? I mean, we have plenty of work here, but I think you might give some folks apoplexy if you waited on them."

Thinking of his valet's words, he said, "I have an idea, if you'd care to hear it, and I welcome your thoughts on how to implement it."

Chapter Eight

Evie had been careful to stay out of sight during the duke's and marquess's visit, keeping her head down when she could not avoid their presence. On the second day, as they were saying their farewells in the front hall, the Duke of Cranbrook glanced at her then snapped his head around to look a second time. But when she quickly ducked into a room, he didn't say anything to Lord Rutland.

When her employer had questioned her, he had believed her story that she'd gained her wisdom working in a London home. She'd worried he'd question it, but it seemed he was either that ignorant of the gap between the aristocracy and their servants or that desperate for assistance regarding his new world.

She could not have planned a better way to evaluate him as marriage material than spending a few hours a day helping him. As a bonus, she no longer had to cast surreptitious glances as she worked to admire his physique. If anything, her aunt had understated his uniqueness. The man was built like no duke she'd ever seen. He could be one of those pugilists so popular in London these days. His shoulders were twice the width of hers, above a trim waist and tree trunks for legs. 'Twas a good thing this duke could afford bespoke clothes, as no ready-made trousers would fit his proportions. Between all that, his arresting face, and that damned throat hollow that beckoned her, she worried she would not be able to focus on the laws which heretofore had been her highest priority.

She raced through her duties the next morning, having a rough idea of his schedule. He generally read papers and ledgers until he was so confused and frustrated he couldn't focus, only to take a quick break before calling in Munroe to go over his questions. Afterwards, he either walked or rode some of his agitation away. So, she anticipated him calling for her later in the afternoon.

She was correct. Walking into his office, she dipped into a shallow curtsy. "You rang, Your Grace?"

"Miss Mullens, may I—?" He cleared his throat. "Please sit down."

"See? You're getting the knack of it." She smiled at him as she lowered to a visitor's chair across from him. When one side of his mouth curled up in amusement, she bit back a gasp. For all his rough edges, open-necked shirts, and almost permanent frown, he was breathtaking when he smiled. Her heart might have missed a beat when his cheek creased and his eyes twinkled.

A splendid attribute in a husband, but his leanings in Parliamentary matters and his treatment of women were still to be determined. At least being on his payroll, she'd already crossed off any concerns about how he dealt with servants. If anything, he deferred too much to them, as he had with her the previous day.

He gestured to the largest pile on one side of his desk. "These are items Munroe cannot help me with. Mostly bills from the House of Commons, headed to the House of Lords, I think?"

She nodded.

"And a few invitations. Munroe managed the ones from this region. These are from London."

"Those will continue to flow in. Dukes are in great demand. Their presence at one event can elevate a host or hostess's reputation for an entire Season."

"Why?"

"Because your set is the most powerful in the kingdom, barring the Royal Family." She shrugged.

"But…a party, or dinner?"

"You'd be surprised at how much business is conducted at these social events. Second only to the clubs. I'm guessing Mr. Lancaster informed you which memberships you have inherited?"

"A club?" He thought. "Perhaps it was the place named after a color? Black's?"

She stifled a giggle. "White's. You were close."

He raised a brow. "Are you laughing at me?"

"Oh, that is perfect. A very ducal expression, Your Grace. You should keep that in your repertoire."

His omnipresent frown returned, his jaw ticking. "You're dismissed."

She gulped a breath. Oh dear, he was upset. She would be, too, if she had to learn every aspect of a new life and some servant sat laughing at her lack of knowledge.

She stood to execute a lower curtsy than her first. "Your Grace, I must beg your pardon. 'Tis difficult for me to fathom someone so unfamiliar with all aspects of the aristocracy. However, I was not laughing at you. I would never. I want to help you. The contradiction of black and white was simply amusing. Please. I am sorry."

He leaned back in his chair, folding his arms across

his chest. "Apology accepted. Sit, please. And enough with the curtsies and the Your Graces. I apologize as well. This is frustrating, and so much of it feels pointless. By this time of day, I am often short-tempered. So many rules and prancing around to observe 'etiquette.' Life in the public house was much simpler."

"I can imagine." She was accustomed to the intricacies of society now, but recalled feeling overwhelmed when she'd learned them years ago.

"I cannot promise you I won't snipe at you again, so have patience with me."

"Is that an order, Your—?" she asked cheekily, trying to tease him out of his bad mood. But she stopped on his title. "What shall I call you?"

"Xander, please."

She gasped. Even some of her friends were uncomfortable calling their betrothed by their first names. Here she was, a servant. "I could not!"

He growled.

"Your Gr—my lord. Please. You have asked for my help with learning this…life. Using someone's first name beyond your closest circle is simply not done. By order of familiarity, you should accept Your Grace, Rutland, my lord, and then a nickname or Xander to only your closest circle."

"Blazes. Fine, then. Rutland, I suppose. Might as well become accustomed to answering to it."

"Still not appropriate for someone who works for you, but I understand, er, Rutland. Let's delay the invitations to another day. Perhaps you can sort them by date of the event, and we can prioritize them that way. Have you read the bills?"

"A few of them. I have opinions on them, but I am

worried they will be unpopular given my background. As you say, they might come up at the social gatherings, I wish to avoid saying the wrong thing."

"Understandable, my lord—Rutland." She corrected herself. "Might I take those and read them between now and tomorrow to discuss with you?"

He arched the ducal brow again. "What? You won't know all of them from perusing the title over my shoulder?"

She arched a brow. If he could be snide, so could she. "Perhaps, but I'd rather be certain. 'Tis your reputation on the line."

* * * *

Evie had been sure the duke would have to vouch for her to get reading time, but the housekeeper accepted her need for daylight hours to go through the documents Evie showed her. The senior staff members had accepted the new duke's unconventional method of running the house and adjusted accordingly.

Having been in the household for the better part of a month, Evie was impatient for knowledge to inform her true purpose, and whether or not to encourage the duke to accept the marriage contract. Determined to obtain an inkling of where Xander's thoughts were on some of the more controversial bills, she waited for the household to settle for the night. Once in her nightclothes, she braided her hair for sleep, enjoying the freedom from the infernal, itchy mobcap she had to wear by day. Then, carrying her slippers, she slipped out of her narrow servant's room and down the back stairs, past the first floor with the duke's private quarters and bedchambers for guests, to the ground level. She slid her footwear on before approaching the library. There, she eased inside around the half-open door and aimed for his desk.

She leaned over the desk to light the gas lamp, not quite daring to go around and sit in the duke's chair. Sliding the pile of documents toward her, she looked for his notes. Not finding them, she turned the lamp a shade brighter to search beyond the one pile. She swore he'd had a folio near him on the desk, but it wasn't there.

Fabric rustled behind her.

She spun around, her heart racing.

The duke lolled lengthwise on the settee, shirt untucked, one foot up on the arm, the other on the ground. His arm was thrown up over his head on the arm behind it. And his eyes were open, staring at her.

She bent a knee, beginning a curtsy.

He growled, and she straightened quickly. Nodding, she tried to brazen it out. "Rutland."

"What the hell are you doing?"

Belatedly, she spied the folio laying open on the low table in front of the settee. Devil it.

"I—I thought one bill was missing a page."

"You cannot think I'll believe that you were reading at this time of night. I am quite sure servants are only allotted one candle for their chambers. Frankly, given what I saw, any more would singe the walls, those rooms are so tiny."

Of course, of all the things he'd have mastered, it had to be servants' allotments. She sighed.

"You are correct, sir." His brows twitched at that moniker, but she ignored it. "I did not want to interfere with your day, so I thought I'd look for it now."

He rose and stretched, his dratted open-necked shirt dragging along his muscular torso, before striding over to stand within arm's length.

"Well, now you've interrupted my night." He stared down at her, his eyes pools of darkness in the planes of light and shadow playing over his face. His curls were in even more disarray than by day, and when he scrubbed a hand over his chin, she could hear the rasp of stubble.

Her heart raced, and heat twinged low in her belly. She licked her lips.

His gaze dropped to her mouth, eyelids remaining lowered. His Adam's apple bobbed.

The heat pouring off him singed her through her nightrail and wrapper, and she shivered.

"Are you cold?" he asked.

She shook her head, unable to form words. Whether that was from fear of being caught in a lie or distraction due to physical turmoil, she did not care to decide.

"Right, then. You owe me a forfeit for awakening me."

"I did you a favor, sir. Your bed must be more comfortable than the settee." Her forwardness, no matter what her position, in mentioning a man's bed made her squirm. Or perhaps it was due to his naked forearms beneath rolled-up sleeves.

"That bed is ridiculously large. Especially when, for some reason, there is a separate set of rooms for the duchess."

As much as she wanted to ask to see said bed, she needed to find a balance between flirting and sanity. She tried, "After sharing your thoughts of my accommodations—in your home, I might add—I don't think 'tis very fair to complain about your bed being too large."

He chuckled.

"Perhaps our forfeits negate one another?" she proposed hopefully. Worry over what her forfeit might be had begun to cloud her thoughts. They might be on totally different pages for what they'd like to explore this evening.

"I don't think so."

She swallowed through a tight throat. "What, then?"

"What do you suggest?" He frowned. "What do other households have as punishment?"

She'd heard her mother discussing such a thing with the housekeeper once, but with him so close, she could not pull the memory forward. Offering a few guesses, she said, "Docking their pay? Forfeiting their day off?"

His lips flattened. "Sounds harsh. What do the London ladies forfeit?"

It would be inexcusably forward of her, but no one had to know. Unable to resist his lure, she dropped her gaze to his hard jaw and lush lips and whispered, "Kisses."

His nostrils flared on a sharp inhale, and he cupped her jaw with a broad work-roughened hand. "That seems more fair."

Her eyelids fluttered, the heat of his hand searing a path from her cheek to between her legs. *Oh my, he is potent.*

His voice was rougher and lower than normal when he asked, "Do you agree?"

Her conscience and newly awakened desire were warring. *You mustn't. But—for husband research.* Unable to resist his heat, his gaze, and his touch, she nodded against his hold.

Before her next breath, his lips were on hers.

Chapter Nine

Xander swooped in as soon as her head moved in the affirmative and set his lips to hers. Taking advantage of her open mouth, he ran his tongue over her bottom lip. As he did, North's voice was shouting alarms in his head. She was in his employ. This was a terrible idea.

He'd fallen asleep on the settee, recalling their interplay of the past several days and wishing they'd met under different circumstances.

He'd woken to her silhouette in full definition, her nightwear all but invisible with the gas lamp backlighting her. Realizing it wasn't a dream when she did not immediately draw close and drop to her knees to suck his iron-hard cock, he rose and prowled toward her, looking for an excuse to touch her.

She gave it to him.

But her response was passive, her lips tentatively mimicking his, and he had to tease at her tongue to get it to come out and play.

Never say she's innocent. He'd never met a working-class girl who wasn't already an expert kisser. Of course, he couldn't speak to the majority, as most girls were married by the twenty-odd years Evie appeared to have lived. He never messed around with married women. But the single ones had had their share of experimenting with kisses, if not more.

A mental alarm pinged. Not about her innocence, but

about her guilt. Regardless of her experience with men, he'd caught her snooping in his office, and he did not give any credit to her paltry excuse.

He shouldn't be so attracted to this little liar.

Without breaking the kiss, he slid the hand holding her cheek around to cup her head and brought the other one to her hip. He stepped one foot between hers and pressed his hips inward, then groaned when her belly cushioned his cock.

She tore her mouth away, looking at him with wide eyes. "Your Grace!"

Yep, innocent, and missish besides. Trust her or not, he needed her advice. And North and the dukes were right about the pitfalls of tupping staff. Damn his infernal attraction to her. He needed to avoid scaring her off. Stepping back, he released his hold on her and said, "I beg your pardon, Miss Mullens."

She ran her fingers along her lips.

He turned away, willing his cockstand to abate, and groped for words. "I—it shall not happen again. Please forgive me; I did not mean to take advantage." He gulped and guessed at her biggest concern. "Your position here is safe, you have my word."

She stood where he had left her, still outlined by the lamplight.

He looked away quickly.

"You did not take advantage, sir. I mean, I suppose you did, but it was not entirely unwelcome."

At her words, his gaze shot back to hers. Thank goodness. She had been flirting with him as much as he had with her.

"'Twas…surprising. Overwhelming. And I agree, it should not happen again." She turned away.

He thought he heard "more's the pity" muttered under her breath, but he could not very well ask. A grin threatened, and he pressed his lips flat to stifle it.

"My workday begins early, so I should return upstairs. Good night, my lord."

He smirked. She hadn't prevaricated about returning during the day for the missing pages. The reminder of her deceit sobered him. He'd do well to keep in mind that the little flirt was also a liar and not to be trusted. "Good night, Miss Mullens."

* * * *

"Explain to me how you know so much about Parliament," Xander requested at the start of their meeting the following afternoon, attempting to act like he didn't know how her waist dipped in and her hips flared beneath the loose, ill-cut servant's garb. It was for the best that she was sitting across the desk from him, where much of her was out of sight.

"I know nothing about process and procedure. You shall have to ask the other dukes about that, or friends you make in London at the start of the session. As for the content, I know what I read in the newspapers and what I've heard discussed in my past roles."

"Do most housemaids read the newspapers, then?"

Evie narrowed her gaze. "About as much as bartenders, I suppose. Some do, some don't."

He winced. Sure, he could have stayed more abreast of happenings in his country and the capital. 'Twas simply that Northumberland was nigh a week from London, at the northernmost point of England before one crossed into Scotland. And most of these laws did not affect his daily life.

However, the more he read, the more he realized how many working-class people *were* affected by these bills and how poorly they were represented in the country's government. He had begun to form a silent plan to use whatever leverage he had to move toward reform for working conditions for many of his peers. Well, perhaps his ex-peers? His head hurt again.

"Right, then. So Insolvent Debtors Act expansion to Ireland, good." He put it aside.

She jerked her head back. "You're going to trust my thoughts on it?"

"I didn't see the original one, but this is progress at the very least. And yes." He watched her calmly. He couldn't explain why, but he trusted her opinion on these. Besides, as a servant, wouldn't her interests align with his?

"You should not." She narrowed her gaze. "You should have a rough idea of what each bill does and its merits and weaknesses. What if its goal was to put all debtors in gaol?"

"I read enough to know that is not the case. I am prioritizing as you suggested." He arched a brow. "Now, what about the Steam Engine Furnaces Act?"

She looked like she wanted to say more regarding his trust in her.

He leaped forward. "Can you summarize the issue, please?" At her glance, he adopted a faux stern visage and growled, "Summarize the issue at once." He grinned, sharing the joke with her.

She caught her breath, looking taken aback, making him wonder if it had been too much, before she returned his smile.

"Certainly, Your—Rutland. They've already been

deemed nuisances when not properly vented or situated too close to neighboring properties. This allows affected people to pursue remedies through the courts without having to pay all those fees; instead, it mandates that the offender pays the costs of litigation and prosecution, as well as any remedies."

Slicing a hand through the air, he said, "Why is there a question around this? They are terrible pollutants, and the explosions are known to be dangerous."

"The Tories would tell you the law impinges on the rights of a landowner. *He*"—she accented the pronoun, and her lips twisted for a moment—"should be able to do what he likes on his property." She scratched at the edge of her cap, something he'd seen her do a few times.

Staring at her, he realized he'd only seen her hair by candlelight and only once. "Remove the cap."

Straightening, she brought wide eyes to his. "I beg your pardon?"

"It seems to annoy you. I've seen you tug at it several times now."

Her face flamed.

"Take it off. I don't know its purpose, but you will not get dust in your hair, or hair in food, or whatever else. You don't need it for this work, so there is no reason to be uncomfortable."

"If Your Grace commands…" she said with a grin, her tone teasing.

He blew out a breath. They were back to their easy camaraderie, their partnership. His transgression last night in demanding a kiss was forgiven, if not forgotten.

She raised her hands to her cap, tugging two pins out.

He sucked in a new gulp of air and held it. Was it the color of her brows, a cinnamon? Lighter? Darker?

She yanked off the cap, and sure enough, cinnamon-colored hair pulled back into a serviceable bun framed her face. One curling lock fell forward by her ear at that moment.

He wanted to tug on it, put it in his mouth and taste it, wrap it around his finger. Seeing his hand start to reach across the desk, he stopped the unconscious motion.

She hadn't noticed his fascination as she smoothed her hair back from her face, grimacing when her hand encountered the wayward curl. Reaching for a discarded pin, she tucked the hank into the knot at the back of her head and heaved a sigh of relief.

How had she dealt with similar head apparel all these years? Perhaps she had not worn a cap in her last post, and perhaps she had only been working for a year or two.

She'd leaned forward while he pondered her aversion to millinery, tilting her head to look at the next document. He was brought back to the issues at hand when she commented, "Another duty law. You'd think they'd learn."

"What do you think they should learn?" he asked.

"If they keep taxing imports and territories under their control, they'll end up driving them away as they did the American colonies."

"What would you suggest?"

"I don't know. Girls are taught more about hostessing than about history, sadly. But I'd guess there are some MPs who have suggestions. 'Tis a reason to spend some time in London."

He shuddered. "I hate that place so much."

"I wonder if once you were more familiar with it and met some like-minded people, it mightn't be so terrible?"

"Perhaps, but how much would I have to endure to get to that point?"

"Your experience might also be different as a duke than a pub manager."

"I wasn't a pub manager. I was helping my stepbrother set up a charitable organization. Yet the men we were trying to help treated me like a servant." Frustration fizzed through him at the memory. "Frankly, being treated differently due to a title I did not earn would aggravate me more."

He sighed. So many pros and cons for each decision, and hundreds of peoples' futures affected by each one. He hadn't wanted this responsibility. Indeed, it frightened him. It was time for a break.

Leaning back in his chair, he rested his elbows on the armrests and put his palms together, worrying his lips between his forefingers as he contemplated this. When he looked up, Evie was staring at his mouth, unblinking.

Dropping his hands, he watched as her gaze flew to meet his. She blushed and lowered her chin to peruse the bill.

Interesting. If only he hadn't promised her he wouldn't kiss her again. Perhaps he could tempt her into initiating a kiss, maybe not now, but over time. Then he'd know he wasn't taking advantage of their positions.

Bringing his hands back up near his mouth, he interlaced his fingers, folding all but the forefingers. He lowered his gaze only as far as he could keep her in his peripheral vision and toyed with his lip. Brushing it, tugging on it.

She was riveted. Her tongue swept across her lips, followed by her teeth sinking into one side of her lower lip.

His cock thickened and lengthened. There would be no relief this afternoon, but he could build on this to coax a kiss from her. His tongue came out to play, moistening his lips.

She squirmed in her chair.

Perfect. "Thank you, Miss Mullens. That is all my brain can handle for one day. Please take another few items to read if you can."

He was going to need some privacy to recover from this—or rather, recall it in intimate detail while giving himself some relief.

Chapter Ten

A few days later, the pile of correspondence still waiting to be addressed was noticeably smaller, and Evie had watched Xander fill page after page of his folio with notes. She was gratified that he was taking the dukedom seriously and elated that he showed no signs of Tory leanings.

However, she was struggling each day to fight her desire for the still-rough-around-the-edges lord. His habit of toying with his lip while thinking was beyond distracting. She wanted nothing more than to round the desk, sit on his lap, and soothe the poor overworked lip— with her tongue. But it would be wrong to kiss him again without confessing her true identity and inappropriate besides. More importantly, he might bar her from the household, given what she'd heard about other maids making advances. She wouldn't mind not having to clean such a large house, but she was trying to make a decision about a person she'd spend the rest of her life with, and she needed more time.

On the other hand, more kissing would help determine compatibility, at least on one level. Perhaps she could entice him into initiating another kiss.

With that in mind, she did not change into her nightrail but removed her cap, leaving her hair loose. She lounged on her narrow bed for an hour after the staff supper, which happened after the duke's repast was complete.

She descended the front stairs this time, hoping the housekeeper did not catch her. By using those stairs, she'd walk right past the library door on her path to the kitchen door to the garden. If Xander happened to notice her, he might follow.

That's His Grace to you. Remember your station. She didn't care what her alter ego wanted her to call him; she craved another taste.

Tossing her hair, she checked that the front door had already been locked for the night and the footman was gone from his post. She was free to step with a little more force, to hold her skirts from hitting the wall and perhaps swish them as much as the fewer layers of servant's garb would allow.

The library door was ajar, and the light was on. If Xander had already stretched out on the settee, he might not see her, but if he was still hunched over his desk, she'd cross in his direct line of sight; he need only look up.

Blast, he was not at his desk. Deflated, she released her skirts and almost turned around. No, she'd go walk the gardens anyway to get some fresh air and time with her thoughts.

Glancing back to see if he was in the library, her breath caught. He stood one step over from the settee, as though he'd risen and moved to see who was in the hall.

Arching a brow at him, she allowed a small smile, cast her sight down the length of him, and casually sauntered toward the kitchen door.

Sensing rather than hearing him at first, she grinned when a boot heel rang on the hallway's marble floor.

She strolled through the kitchen and took her time

unlatching the portal to the gardens. Not hearing him behind her now, she frowned but continued. He knew where she was. The rest was up to him. In the meantime, she'd enjoy the balmy evening.

Picking an aimless path along the garden walks lit only by the house windows and the moon, she ran her hand lightly over the plants in bloom. Vegetables first, then, as she neared the side of the house and ventured farther from the kitchen, flowers of all types with a preponderance of roses. Pricking her finger on a thorn, she paused her wanderings to suck it into her mouth.

A click from the house came, a swish, then the duke was striding off the low veranda from the balcony doors in his library.

Her pulse ticked faster. In the inevitable open-necked, cravatless shirt and trousers, he appeared huge. Broad shoulders and shaggy hair blocked the light from the room behind him, leaving his expression in darkness.

Perhaps he was annoyed and would ask her to go inside.

A single shiver ran through her. If only she were there as herself, Lady Evelyn, she could refuse and force him to carry her inside if he wanted her there. But she was a maid, subject to his whim. She could only hope his whims included touching. Allowing that mindset to settle over her, she swallowed the saliva that pooled in her mouth as she assessed his charms.

He stopped a foot from her, closer than etiquette between peers allowed. He shifted to one side, and the light hit her face, making her squint. Peering up at him, she licked her lips.

He sucked in a sharp inhale. "What are you doing out here at night, without even a candle?"

"A candle would blow out in the breeze, and there is enough light that I can see my way. I wanted to enjoy some fresh air and quiet."

"Ah." He nodded once. "Should I leave you to it, then?"

'Twas the perfect opportunity. "My lord, this"—she gestured with a wide flung arm—"is yours to command. As am I."

It was his turn to shudder then. His voice was a rumble of distant thunder when he replied, "'Tis past working hours. And anyway, I cannot command what I want you to do."

"Why not?" she asked, her voice husky.

"'Twould not be right."

"No one is here. Tell me, my lord. If you were not concerned with right or wrong, what would you have me do?" She took a half step closer, provoking him. But she'd been a lady far longer than she'd been a maid, and ladies did not initiate kisses. Or did they? She might have to ask her friends about that when she returned to London.

"Nay, I cannot answer that. It would be tantamount to the command itself." Yet he hadn't retreated to maintain space between them.

She was a maid now, not a lady. Might as well take advantage of the freedom. She licked her lips again.

A satisfying gasp escaped from him.

She leaned in, so close her breath gusted over his tieless neck as she asked in a whisper, "Shall I guess?"

Not waiting for an answer, she gripped his upper arm—goodness, that was hard—and went on tiptoe to slant her lips over his.

His hands settled above her hips, and he sighed into

her mouth, "Thank God."

Her fingers flexed into his granite biceps, and she gave herself over to the kiss. For long moments, his tongue played with hers, his lips alternating pressure with softness. Roaming hands along her back brought every inch of her skin to life. Her nipples peaked—they might be as hard as his arm muscles—and she pressed full, sensitive breasts against him.

He tugged her hair, still in its bun, to continue the kiss, and her free hand came up to explore his chest through his thin lawn shirt. He surged against her, his hardness poking her in the belly through their clothing.

Their magnetism boded well for a marriage. Her thoughts fractured and exploded into confetti when he cupped her breast in an outsized, rough hand and swiped a thumb across her nipple.

Her hands on his arm and chest clenched to hold her up as her knees buckled from the shot of lightning that pierced her from nipple to the swollen folds between her legs.

He caught her weight with his other arm, sliding it across to band behind her back. When he intensified the pressure of his lips, she leaned back under the onslaught.

Apparently, that was what he wanted, as he broke off the kiss and replaced his thumb's strokes with the suction of his mouth on her tight bud.

"Xander!" she cried, ignoring protocol. If he was going to take such liberties with her body, he could not object to her doing the same with his name. She threaded her fingers through his hair and gripped his head, uncertain if she wanted to yank him away or hold him there forever.

Her most private flesh pulsed, and she felt a rush of

wetness. She had read enough and had enough married girlfriends that she knew her body was readying itself for his touch. And oh, did she want it. She wished to explore all the benefits that wedding and bedding him would bring.

How would she explain her true identity after misleading him for so long?

Feeling as though freezing water had been dumped on her, she gasped and pulled out of his arms. Blast, why could she not be like all those heroines in the novels and be mindless with pleasure? But the risk was too great. If he was angry at her deception and refused to marry her after taking her innocence, she'd be ruined.

He blinked and straightened, and they stared at each other for a long moment.

Finally, she found her voice, taking refuge in formality. "Your Grace, it is my turn to beg your pardon now for taking liberties. I hope you will forgive my transgression."

He opened his mouth to speak, but she hurried on, using her standard excuse. "My workday begins early, so I shall take my leave."

She fled.

* * * *

Evie knelt on the floor, polishing the legs of the small table and chairs in the duke's library, as she did once a week.

He seemed to have forgotten her presence.

She smirked. *Settling right into that dukedom, aren't you?*

Munroe sat in front of his desk as Xander worked his way through a new pile of contracts he'd found in a drawer.

Taking meals with staff had introduced her to more bawdiness than even her married friends had shared, including the phrase "polishing his knob" from the male servants. His gesture had clarified his meaning. Now, as she polished the duke's knobs of wood, she had to stifle a snort of laughter.

Glancing over, she imagined oiling—another muffled snort—his desk, crawling under it to be thorough. Having him sit there with her at his feet.

Her imagination stalled on that image. She simply did not have the experience to picture what he'd do or want her to do.

Would he be the sort of husband who would teach her? Would he want that from his wife, or was that sort of behavior only among servants? Perhaps that was why she'd never heard the term before. Oh, if only she could visit with her aunt without giving her disguise away. She could not even write letters, as the footman who mailed them would question why a housemaid was writing to ladies and countesses.

She was almost certain she wanted that—

"—marriage contract?!" Xander's voice rose to a near shout as he finished her thought aloud.

"Ah, yes. His Grace had shown me that. I wondered where it had gotten to. I shouldn't worry about it, Your Grace. You have time before the family demands an answer. They spend most of their time in London. Perhaps they will wait until you journey there to discuss the matter in person."

"What is there to discuss?"

"We should review the document, but 'tis my understanding that these contracts include protracted negotiations, and both families are expected to fulfill them with whatever means necessary, as other terms may have already been met. Financial ties linked, other offers declined, that sort of thing?" Munroe waved an uncertain hand.

Evie gritted her teeth. She was not simply another bullet point on a contract, as though she couldn't procure another offer with a few smiles and a wave of her fan.

There might be some stigma if the contract was dropped, but surely, her family could spin it as an uncouth commoner not being worthy of her.

Her heart clenched at that thought. She wanted to choose for herself. But she didn't want Xander's reputation soiled, no matter who declined the union. Blast, it appeared she preferred not to hurt him even if he spurned her. This was a fine fettle of a dilemma she'd not anticipated.

The duke's voice brought her back to the library. "You cannot be serious. I'm expected to wed some Ton chit because of a contract? Someone who is bound to find me beneath her snooty sensibilities?"

He had a point. She was, after all, laboring in disguise to verify his suitability. And she'd had the fleeting thought before meeting him that his humble origins might embarrass her. Hellfire, she should have thought that when she noticed his continued lack of proper dress, but that throat hollow was too alluring to allow such a concern. More, they had fun together, and their politics aligned. He was everything she'd hoped for and fun, besides.

She wished she could laugh at how upside down the whole situation was. The person born to the aristocracy was on her knees polishing the furniture owned by a man raised working-class who now held the highest non-royal title in the land.

"Your Grace," Munroe said in a placating tone. "Take some time to think about it. You need heirs, and 'tis my understanding that this particular young lady is quite genial and comely besides. I believe she is related to someone in the village, too."

Xander sat back in his chair and brought his elbows to the armrests and his fingers to his lips.

She groaned, a spurt of warmth flooding her. Must he?

He frowned and asked, "So I am supposed to marry for geniality, beauty, and heirs? What of love?"

Ohh, good question. She quietly shifted to the floor by another chair so she could see more of his face. Then she frowned. She'd never considered love before. Affection, certainly, but she assumed anything more would grow over time. Until she'd discovered the previous duke's politics, she'd been fine with a society marriage, negotiated and contracted, as all of her peers were. There was no reason she should be leaning on one hand where she knelt to tilt closer and catch every word.

Munroe blushed. She could see it even from where she sat. "I could not speak to that, Your Grace."

"You've never been in love, Munroe? You have, what, a few years on me?"

"I am eight-and-twenty, sir. And no. I take it you have?"

Before the duke could answer, Evie toppled to the floor, narrowly missing the uncapped linseed oil bottle beside her knee. She'd leaned one inch too far. Her elbow hit the wood floor with a crack. "Ouch!"

Both men's heads whipped around.

The duke raised a brow. "Are you quite all right, Miss Mullens?"

"Sorry, sir. Yes, thank you, sir. I'll, ah…" She looked around. "You know, I think I have finished this. I shall go check with Mrs. Betters regarding my next task."

Doing a terrible job at stifling a grin, the duke nodded.

* * * *

Late that afternoon, the duke sent for her again.

Evie had worried all day about what to do if he broached the topic of marriage contracts or, indeed, marriage at all, with her.

Sure enough, as soon as she entered the library, he stood and gestured for her to sit before tossing the contract across the desk.

"Rutland, as a reminder, you needn't stand for a maid," she teased him.

"Oh. Right. Well, better safe than sorry, I suppose." He shrugged and threw himself into his chair. "I'm rattled. As you apparently saw and heard."

She dipped her head.

"What do you know of marriage contracts?"

"I doubt I know much more than you, sir. My understanding is that they are negotiated between the patriarchs of the families. Sometimes one of them is the future husband; sometimes the poor tyke isn't even in short pants yet."

"What if they hate each other?" His burning gaze shifted from the hated contract to her.

She folded her arms. How to answer that? "You grew up expecting to work in a tavern. I'll wager when you started, it felt somewhat natural."

He nodded. His expression smoothed, and he tilted his head.

She hoped she could get him to see it from her point of view. "A duke, or even a baron, would likely find it tremendously difficult, however. They wouldn't have lifted anything heavy or worked the same hours. But as you had anticipated it, you could adapt more easily."

"I understand what you're saying, but this is not a position that you can leave and go home every night."

"Isn't it, though? First, did you go home? Didn't you tell me you'd lived above the public house and were the person on call for deliveries and emergencies?"

"Well, yes, but I was still able to separate myself most of the time."

"Isn't there an entire separate suite of rooms above stairs for your duchess?"

He glowered at her. "Us pub workers expect to sleep with the woman we marry, to enjoy the benefits that come with marriage."

Heat rushed to her cheeks. "My lord! 'Tis inappropriate to speak of such things in mixed company."

He arched a brow and asked, "Even with a servant?"

She paused. She didn't know the answer to that. "Better safe than sorry."

"Ha! Well played, Evie," he capitulated, grinning.

She exhaled a sigh of relief at his reaction. Butterflies fluttered in her stomach at his first use of her given name.

"I don't want to marry a stranger." His words squashed the butterflies, and she stiffened as he continued. "Everything I have learned so far is that dukes control not only their own lives but practically the entire country. I would never have imagined that the most important choice of all would not be their own."

She heaved a happy sigh. How romantic to call it the most important decision. *Stay on topic, Evie.* He had a point. Even she'd had a say in whom she'd marry.

He continued, "I seem to recall North choosing his first wife as well as Mama. And the Duke of Cranbrook said he'd chosen his. Hmm. Munroe mentioned that I should speak to him about this. Perhaps I'll do that. There seems to be a real possibility that I shall have to go to London to meet this chit's family. What else do I need to know before I dive into that den of iniquity?"

Her eyes rounded. "So much. There are seating etiquettes and introductory proprieties and appropriate supper conversation topics. I am not sure where to start. Oh, and dancing."

"Dancing?" His eyes widened.

She nodded.

"Do you dance?"

She nodded again.

"Excellent. And do you know enough about all the etiquette nonsense you just spouted to at least get me started?"

She nodded, frantically trying to think of a reason a servant would know that.

He didn't ask. "Then you'll join me at dinners henceforth, and I'll see about getting some musicians here as soon as possible."

Where would he find musicians? Oh, but she hoped he did. Dancing 'twas a perfect excuse to become better acquainted with his thick, sturdy frame.

Chapter Eleven

After some convincing—"'tis just not done!"—Banks had agreed that Xander could help with deliveries at the public house before hours when he had time, but preferably with notice so that Banks could give one or more of his workers the day off, with pay, of course.

As for having a meal and a drink, Banks suggested easing the other pub-goers into things as Frazer had. Perhaps a drink in a corner of the room or at the end of the bar, and the meal in the private dining room or, if it wasn't busy, in Banks' office with the proprietor joining him. Then they could ease him into spending longer at the bar in a few weeks.

Heeding their concerns, Xander had agreed and had already spent three evenings lurking in a dark corner of the public room, nursing an ale and fielding questioning looks and deferential nods. Happily, the quizzical looks had become shorter and shorter before the other patrons went about their business.

Those occasional mornings and evenings had saved his sanity. Focusing on physical labor and watching people who performed it all day reminded him to wield his new power for the good of the majority of the country, not those who held money and power and wanted to retain it. On the other hand, it made him miss his simpler life in a new way. If he wasn't a duke, he wouldn't need to marry, and he could tup whom he pleased, including a maid with gorgeous reddish-brown hair hidden under a mobcap.

Having sent the requisite note after his conversation with Evie, Xander was in the back alley bright and early the next morning. If anyone knew where to find musicians on short notice, Banks would.

Sure enough, Banks had a few ideas and told him he'd send a note over after he'd made a few inquiries. By the midday meal, Xander had musicians scheduled to arrive after supper.

The meal itself was frustrating. Before he was even allowed to sit down, Evie called him to find the long dining table set as though for a dozen guests. He was given placards with names on them, only half of which he recognized, and she led him around the table, indicating where each would sit and why.

She'd been kind enough to include his mother and stepfather, but not his brother. But with the duke and the marquess who had visited among the names, his parents were seated several chairs down from his seat at the head of the table, which made no sense to him.

"Why is my brother not among these names?"

Evie gulped. "Your brother is…problematic."

Xander frowned in confusion. "You've never met him. He's a lot nicer than I am by most people's standards."

"The Ton do not welcome…illegitimate relations at a formal dinner."

He stared. She was joking, wasn't she? She must be. There would never be a house of his that did not welcome Bruce to all social events within it. Finally, he said, "Do you know where he'd sit if I ignored etiquette and included him? Never mind, I suspect I know. It would be the farthest end of the table from me, with the lowest-ranked guests."

She nodded, her hands clasping and unclasping in front of her.

"'Tis quite all right, Evie. You do not make the rules. I'll make a note of it. That is not where Bruce will sit at any dinner I host."

Moving on quickly, she cleared the other settings away and sat to his left—where his mother might sit if she had been duchess before him, or where his own duchess would one day sit. There were more sets of utensils surrounding his plate than he'd ever seen, and she'd organized an eight-course meal with the kitchen.

Finally, the whole ordeal was done. Mentally exhausted from all the rules around dining, he stood, needing a moment to steady himself with the back of his chair. Eight courses came with a similar increase in wine consumption. While he could hold his liquor with the best of them after working at a pub these past years, he wasn't sure he was up to dancing after consuming so much liquid and food. But the musicians had arrived, and he needed to be prepared should a request from his potentially betrothed's family come.

Gesturing for Evie to precede him, he stepped into the hall to the sound of string instruments warming up.

Evie turned to him in surprise, and he wanted to lean down and lick her parted lips. Right, then. No more wine for him.

"You found musicians *in a day*?" she asked.

He shrugged and tried to make light of it. "I'm a duke."

She snorted.

He snorted.

They both broke out in laughter there in the hall, pausing in place because they could not see to walk.

Finally, she sobered enough to say, "Shall we dance, then?"

He held his arm out for her and led her into the music room.

* * * *

As they waited for the musicians to finish tuning their instruments, he turned to Evie and gestured. "Take the cap off?"

She shrugged and quickly removed it, placing it on a narrow table by the door before unpinning her hair as well.

He gulped a swallow.

She asked, "What dances do you know?"

"A few country dances, and a reel."

She tapped her lip with a finger. "Then you should learn the quadrille, perhaps the cotillion. And the newest dance, although not included at the more formal balls, is the waltz."

"Why would certain dances be excluded?"

"The waltz has not been accepted by the society matrons. They consider it very risqué." She widened her eyes in mock horror.

"Why?" he asked with a head tilt.

"I assume because the dance partners remain in one pair the whole dance, and they dance rather close."

He grimaced. "Given that I don't know it, that sounds somewhat dangerous to my partner."

She chuckled. "If you can dance the livelier dances and weave between partners, you'll be fine with the new dance." Stepping toward him, she said, "Let us practice without music for a moment. This one follows three-quarter time and has a basic box step."

He sidled closer, uncertain. His trousers went tight as his shaft showed no such uncertainty in wanting to brush against her.

She raised her right hand out at almost shoulder height. "There are several hand positions, but for now, we'll start with one. Give me your hand here, with the other at the same height, bent elbow, hand near my shoulder."

His brows rose, but he did as she said, his cock continuing to lengthen and harden in his trousers.

She sucked in a breath at the touch of his hand on her arm.

That touch—so close to a lady's torso and possibly on skin depending on the length of her gloves—must be the reason the dance was deemed inappropriate for polite company. As he stood, her skin warm under his hand through her dress and her small fingers wrapping around his other hand, he understood why. Any closer and she'd feel his body's reaction.

Her left hand came to his bent arm, and both their gazes followed it. Her hand appeared tiny against his sleeve. His biceps flexed in reaction to her touch, and he saw and felt her fingers clench in an infinitesimal squeeze as they dug into his hard muscle.

She shifted a half inch closer to set her feet in line with his and he nearly reared back, worried his cock might poke her.

Nodding to him, she seemed oblivious when she said, "Watch my feet and follow them with yours."

Taking him through the basic waltz steps, she kept their "boxes" of steps all facing one direction for several counts. Then she showed him a basic quarter turn. After a few circles and squares, she stopped them and dropped her hands.

Cool air wafted over him. He blinked, missing her smiling face so near, her skin against his roughened hand, the hot brand of her other hand on his arm.

She said, "Generally, of course, you shall lead. However, I can lead the first few times if you'd prefer."

"I'm willing to try. I might as well start as I mean to go on."

She called to the musicians to play something in three-fourths time, keeping it slow. They nodded and conferred, then set their bows to their instruments.

Stepping back to him as the first notes rang out, she curtsied. He caught on quickly and bowed. She raised her arms.

He met her frame, relishing the return of the contact. Damn, he loved her hair, even scraped back into a severe knot. Stepping forward and into the dance, he tried to keep her gaze, only glancing down when he made the quarter turns to rotate them and move around the floor.

She smiled. "You're doing so well, Rutland. You are a quick study in this, as with everything."

His hand had a mind of its own and began to stray along her back, creating a subtle but inexorable draw toward him. Feeling the knobs of her spine, he rubbed his first two fingers along them. If only she was wearing a proper ballgown and not a simple maid's dress. Then he'd be able to caress her skin and pull her closer, proper frame be damned.

Her mouth opened on an inhale and her tongue flicked out to wet her lips. After a long moment, she admonished him, "Your hand should remain on my upper arm, your elbow out, so I can cling to your biceps…"

He thought she murmured, "…not that I can find purchase."

However, the music prevented him from being sure. Smiling, he lifted his arm. The scent of lemon verbena used in the cleaning products she worked with daily rose to his nostrils. Her thick hair the color of oiled mahogany begged for him to rub his face along the shiny tresses, bury his nose in it, and wrap it around his fingers to tug on it.

She gasped.

Without conscious thought, he'd tightened their stance further, his hand now pressing into her back and his feet offset with hers. Their hips brushed with each step, her skirts swaying against his legs when she followed him in a step. When they turned, his cock rubbed along her, urging him to lower her to the floor.

"My lord, you are too close."

"Blazes, I'm not close enough." He halted, the music flowing around them. Stroking her gorgeous hair, he tilted her head and took advantage of her open-mouthed gaze. His lips met hers, his tongue plundering as he tugged her close enough that her breasts brushed his shirt.

The music screeched to an abrupt halt.

She remained silent.

He took it as assent, at least for more kisses.

Raising his head, he turned to the musicians. "Can you return tomorrow evening?"

"Certainly, Your Grace."

"Thank you. Rogers will see you out." Not releasing her hand, he tugged her out of the room and down the hall to the library.

Closing and locking the door, he assessed her expression. "Now, where were we?"

"Dancing?"

"No, no, I distinctly recall a different activity. Perhaps I must spark your memory." He leaned against the door, drawing her between his legs with a gentle hand, giving her every opportunity to withdraw or protest. At her acquiescence, his heart soared. He wanted this girl. It had nothing to do with his recent abstinence, her warmth against him, or the dancing, although that last might have precipitated this moment.

Her intellect, her willingness to help him, and her beautiful silky hair were what drew him.

He inclined his head, and she met him halfway. Exploring the wet heat of her mouth, the rough edges of her teeth, and the answering thrust of her tongue made him growl. One hand fisted in her hair, holding her to him. The other stroked her back, retracing the bumps of her spine and the muscles running alongside, then her side, edging closer to her bust.

She arched against him, her hands clinging to his upper arms, fingers flexing and straightening against him.

His hips thrust an inch involuntarily as he imagined that motion against his cock. He slowly traced a blunt fingernail along the modest neckline of her dress, signaling where he planned to go next. Her reactions to date had told him she was more innocent than any maid—hell, any woman—he'd met in his previous life.

Loosening his hold on her chignon without releasing it, he softened his kiss and trailed his hand down from her décolletage to cup her breast.

Gasping into his mouth, she tore her lips away to gape at him, chest heaving against his hand.

Chapter Twelve

Evie could not think. She could only react, her heart racing, every inch of her pressing into Xander. His hand in her hair felt like the sweetest form of possession. His touch on her breast was foreign and new and the best thing she'd ever felt. Her skin tingled and her feminine parts throbbed, begging for something more.

His roving hand cupped her breast, and her knees liquified. Worried she'd faint, she pulled free from his kiss, gasping for breath but careful not to pull the rest of her back.

Because that touch was everything. Fire raced through her, but she did not know what to ask for. The searing heat of his hand had her needing to strip her dress down, to feel his skin against hers, perhaps even his lips there.

She wanted to do the same to him and gauge his reaction.

Unable to form words, she stared at him.

He watched her, still leaning against the door, his hands still and his touch light.

He was asking for permission, she realized. Swallowing, she gazed down at his hand against her dress, then up at his face. Managing only one word, she said in a husky voice, "More."

One side of his mouth curled into a half smile. Entranced, she wasn't prepared for another hot lick of fire when his thumb swiped across her pebbled tip. She gasped again and arched into his hand.

"You say how much more. I'll stop when you tell me." His voice held gravel.

With that, he swept her up and carried her across the room. Putting her on her feet next to the settee, he spun her to untie the apron worn over her simple dress, yanking it away to drop to the floor. His hands pressed her onto the seat then again to urge her to lie down.

He came down over her, a knee between her legs with the other on the edge of the seat cushion, an elbow squeezing between her shoulder and the back of the sofa.

She reached for him, taking her cue from his earlier actions. Threading her fingers through his hair, she reveled in the sheer amount of it. Her fingers disappeared beneath the thick pelt. He groaned, she hoped in pleasure. Her other hand slid up his chest to grasp his shoulder again. When he canted his hips to rest on hers, the heat of him spread through her from everywhere they touched.

He made fast work of the top two buttons of her serviceable dress and pressed his lips to the opening.

Her nails dug into his scalp and muscle. The velvet of his lips sent a flaming arc through her that settled between her thighs where a rigid bar pressed.

He explored every inch of exposed flesh, his hand pressing the mound of her breast up to reach further under her dress with his lips and tongue. As he retraced the column of her neck to her mouth with his, his hand on her breast continued to build the fire he'd sparked.

Without conscious thought, she mimicked his movements. Her hands explored his arms, shoulders, and back. Lingering at his waist, she wished to feel that delicious, muscled arse that was shown off so well in his tighter aristocratic trousers. But she wasn't quite that daring yet.

His hips pressed into hers, grinding that iron shaft against her.

She shifted, and a lightning bolt of pleasure shot through her when his thrusts hit a sensitive spot.

"Rutland—Xander!"

"There, eh?" He gentled his movements, making them smaller and faster.

"Oh!"

Rising over her on one arm, he tugged her skirts upward. They were caught between his knee and the settee, so he pushed up on his toes to yank at it.

Her mouth went dry as she caught sight of his arm muscles bulging against his shirt. She'd never been so glad for his informal dress.

He shifted to put both knees between hers and tunneled his hand under the skirt he'd freed.

Roughly calloused hands scraped along her inner thigh, shocking more nerves into awareness. She gasped. "What are you doing?"

"This will be even better without clothes, I promise."

"But—but—"

He stilled. "I won't hurt you. I promise. Or if you want me to stop, I will."

Did she want him to stop?

"What about if you let me try, then I'll stop and check in with you?"

Yes, that seemed like an excellent idea. She'd needed a minute to think or at least catch her breath, and he was offering that.

She nodded.

"Thank *Christ*." He was straddling her leg now, his hand at the crease of her thigh, tugging on the coarse curls covering her most secret place.

A place that was quite wet. Before she could find embarrassment, his fingers threaded along her swollen folds, pressing them as though plumping and opening them.

"Damnation, you are so wet, sweetling. Is that all for me?" he said with a huge grin.

Well, then. Apparently, that was a good thing.

He parted her lips and pressed a finger against a spot that twisted pleasure and so much sensation it bordered on pain. She grabbed his forearm and breathed, "Xander."

"I have you. Do you want me to stop?"

"It feels…scary? Overwhelming?"

"Not scary. I've got you. 'Twill be all right. It can be overwhelming in the nicest possible way. Have you never touched yourself here?"

She shook her head and shrugged. "In the bath."

"Well, you can try it sometime as well, but it is usually more pleasurable with someone else involved. Now—" He crooked his finger the tiniest bit over that nub and she gasped again and clenched her hands on his arm. "—shall I check in with you every ten strokes?"

She nodded furiously, unsure if she was floating on waves of pleasure or on fire. The settee below her had disappeared. The only thing she perceived was his fingers. Right *there*. She saw only his exultant gaze as he watched her expressions and reactions. His fingers shifted again, back and forth, circles, and her eyes closed, unable to use any senses except experiencing his touch. Her hand still gripped his arm, but now it was as a lifeline rather than to stop him.

Pressure and pleasure built, the threat of pain falling away as she became accustomed to his caresses. Tendrils of sensation climbed from their point of contact like vines, up her torso to curl around her breasts and harden her nipples against her chemise.

Suddenly, it all stopped. His forefinger dropped to toy with her womanly opening and that created a budding ecstasy all its own. But that, too, stopped after a few prods.

"Xander," she gasped, opening her eyes to plead with him. "Please."

"More?"

Lord above, he'd said he'd check in every ten strokes. "More."

His thumb slid against her nub, newly wetted with her moisture. Ah, gads, she was going to explode. If he stopped again before she understood where this was leading, she might kill him. Panting, she begged, "Don't…stop…"

He didn't; instead, he sped up.

Every muscle in her body clenched. Evie keened through teeth clamped together as her flesh quivered and imploded, those vines of sensation constricting her organs and limbs to squeeze out every ounce of pleasure. Gasping for air, she tightened her legs around his hand as fire flashed through her and her nails dug into his arm through his shirt. She didn't know whether she wanted to keep him where he was or yank his arm away.

When it all became too much, he gentled his touch, slowed, and stilled.

"Magnificent, Evie. Thank you for allowing me the pleasure of giving you pleasure."

Her eyes fluttered open in time to watch him tug his hand out of her clothes and raise it to his mouth to suck the fingers that had been on her most intimate parts. Another streak of fire flashed in her belly.

He smirked at her wide eyes then straightened her skirts. His hands took one last caress over her exposed breast and unbuttoned dress before he leaned back to allow her to right herself.

He'd thanked her, when she should be thanking him. How very undukelike. But exactly what she wanted in a husband.

Now that he'd taught her some pleasures of the marriage bed, she couldn't think of a reason to delay indulging them. She'd worry about how to tell him who she was later.

Chapter Thirteen

That fancy wine-colored couch would now forever hold a place of honor in his library. By all that's holy, his fingertips might be singed from the heat of his gorgeous little maid.

He'd be willing to bet the duke's coffers that was her first orgasm—ever, not just at his hand. And he'd gotten to taste it.

Upstairs in bed, Xander drifted off to sleep with his fingers by his nose. He didn't care to toss one off, although there had been a point in the library when he thought he might explode without a touch simply from her softness, wetness, and essence. Seeing her pleasure, feeling it against his fingers, was more than enough satisfaction for him, at least for the time being.

He hoped she wouldn't panic and do something drastic like quit her position in the morning. If that happened, he'd try to talk her into staying. But from what he'd seen, the young woman had mettle. Indeed, she—a housemaid—was training a duke. So perhaps it would all be fine.

And indeed it was. As he crossed the hall from breakfast, he saw her dusting a parson's table in the front hall. His shoes slapped on the marble floor, and she glanced up. After casting a quick look around the space, she ran her eyes up and down his form.

His cock perked up at the attention. Aiming for the

library door quickly so the servants wouldn't be scandalized, he held her gaze. Pausing with a hand on the frame, he winked, enjoyed the resulting blush that stole over her, and continued on his way.

Later that day, as they sat in the library, he couldn't focus on Parliamentary decisions. Instead, the minute Evie walked into the room, he asked, "This marriage contract is somewhat vague about timing. It says at an agreed-upon date once—" he glanced down. "—Miss Allen reaches her majority. And since I don't know the chit, I have no idea when that is or was."

Evie slid onto her usual chair. "Given the circumstances, her family will likely be flexible."

He grumbled, "I'm not ready to marry."

"A wife would leave you more time to handle the management of the dukedom." She gestured at the desk. "She would manage the household and its finances, and all social arrangements—accepting invitations, entertaining guests, and so on."

He blinked. That thought was tempting, but only if she wouldn't drag him to London for months at a time or schedule social engagements every night. However, he only liked the idea when he pictured Evie in the role and not some Ton chit on his arm, in his house, or in his bed.

She tilted her head. "You can't tell me you actually enjoy any of that, Rutland."

"But I'd have veto power?"

"You're a duke. As I've been telling you, there is very little you don't have control over." Her tone was matter of fact. "Why do you ask? She'll have been trained to take your wishes into consideration and ensure your comfort."

He smirked at that last, and she rolled her eyes.

Sobering, his thoughts grew serious. There wasn't a time when he could foresee being able to navigate all this correspondence without Evie's assistance. No wife would be allowed to drive her away. But what if she didn't want to stay? He could not fathom the need for a duchess, whereas Evie was necessary to his happiness, never mind his productivity. "I can't lose you. I need your help with all this, as much or more than I need Munroe."

Her mouth curled in a one-sided smile before she said, "Your betrothed could likely help you in a similar fashion."

"Ha. Have you met any of those society princesses? I'm not sure they can read. Twitter-brains, every single one I ever encountered."

"Really?" she drawled. "And you've had many conversations with society ladies?"

"Well, no. But the ones I encountered on the street and in shops were always prattling about the latest gossip or arguing over whose gown was nicer, oblivious to those of us trying to earn our keep. The more I think about it, the less I like it. All this is a moot point as I doubt I'll marry the Allen girl."

She pursed her lips.

But he was already moving on to the next order of business. Sliding a document from his "decision needed" pile to the center of the desk, he glanced up at her through his lashes. "The Stamps Act?"

"Ugh. Another one? If we must. What are they wanting to tax now?"

"Sounds as though we are against that one." He put it aside.

We? He liked the sound of that.

Chapter Fourteen

Telling Xander her identity should have been her priority, but getting to know him without the pressures of being a titled lady was too satisfying to give up.

She'd slept like the dead after Xander strummed her body to the stars, but in the cold light of early morning, her thoughts became jumbled. She wanted him, of course. Craved that breadth and brawn, that delectable throat hollow, his rough hands and soft lips. But more, she had seen enough of his perspective on the Parliamentary laws and his treatment of those around him that she needed him forever, in fact might already be in love with him.

At that thought, her heart pounded. The stakes in her strategy were higher than she'd ever imagined they'd be.

She ought to speak to her aunt. Aunt Lou always had the best plans, and this one had to be perfect, showing him all the ways she could be his perfect wife without lying to him for so long it would cause irreparable damage. But how to finagle a visit? Louisa was often out and about with friends during the afternoon, and that was when Xander liked to meet with Evie. So she'd ask for a morning off and race to the village and back in a half day. In the meantime, she was going to enjoy her time with him.

As she approached the dining room that evening, a shiver ran through her, and she rubbed her hands together in eagerness. There was a lot of Xander to explore, and perhaps he'd allow her the opportunity to learn his body as he had hers.

When he entered a minute later, and they sat, she explained, "I did not wish to tax Cook's budget or creativity, so we're having the usual three-course 'at home' supper of an aristocratic household. I hope that is all right?"

She was essentially taking on a duchess's role by directing staff about meal planning, while in reality—for the moment—she worked for the housekeeper, as did the chef. But no one questioned her. Perhaps, like the rest of the staff, Cook was deferring to the more casual, respectful approach Xander employed. Or he may have told them to honor her requests. Either way, informing him of what to expect helped prepare him as requested.

"'Tis fine." His response brought her back to the dining room. "Three courses is already too much, given how much less exercise I get these days. Are all dukes overweight?"

She giggled. Indeed, many were. "It varies. Some ride their land to stay fit, particularly as those with tenant farmers need to check on crops and disputes and such. In London, they'd ride in Hyde Park."

"Can I walk it?"

"You can." She drew out the words, doubtful. "Whether you walk or ride, in London you'll be stopped every few feet for social niceties, as 'tis a very popular spot to see and be seen."

His lips twisted in distaste, and she nearly laughed, having anticipated this response. "You get up hours before most of the Ton, my lord, so you'll avoid most of it. And there are other parks."

He grunted.

"Shall I request wine and the start of supper service?" She stopped. "No. You should. 'Tis good practice. Just don't growl at them as you do me when you're being ducal."

He stared, and she went into gales of laughter. "You know what I mean."

His mouth twitched. He raised a hand and took a breath to call a footman. Before he could utter a word, the man was at his side. "Wine, Your Grace?"

Xander blinked, and she had to raise her napkin to hide another grin. Then he replied, "Yes, please, Duncan."

Evie started. She knew the man's name, but rarely did dukes refer to their servants by their first—or even their last name.

When the young man started to pour his wine, the duke growled, despite her directive. The footman stopped, spilling a few drops on the tablecloth. "I'm ever so sorry, Your Grace. Is the wine not to your liking? I can get something else. And I'll clean that up right away."

Xander was frowning. "I haven't tasted the wine, but I'm sure 'tis fine. Serve the lady first, however."

"Ah, no, sir. Duncan had it right. He serves you first as the highest ranked person at the table."

"Not in my house."

She rolled her eyes. "You're going to have to let some of your principles go, you know, so when you host a party in London, it isn't a complete scandal."

"My plebeian sensibilities have no place in a ducal drawing room—or dining room, is that it? I don't care. And I don't plan to host people who do care enough that it would be called a scandal." He gestured. "Now, go ahead, Duncan. Sorry to startle you, and please give my apologies to Jenny."

Again, Evie was shocked he knew who washed laundry for the household.

He caught her expression. "I like to know who is handling my smallclothes, don't you?"

She snorted. Next to her as he poured her wine, Duncan's hand shook, and she heard his stuttered breath as he fought laughter as well.

They reviewed another law as they dined. When she had one last swallow of wine, Evie cleared her throat, needing to tackle a sensitive subject.

"What is it?" Xander was watching her.

"As much as last night was quite enjoyable, you need to learn to dance. And I cannot afford to gain a reputation by you dismissing the musicians a second time."

"They wouldn't dare."

"They wouldn't dare about a duke. But about a young woman alone with him?" She gave a shrug and a wry smile.

He grunted again. She should probably encourage him to stop that, but she rather liked the honesty of his sounds of disgruntlement. There'd be time enough to accomplish the fine polishing.

He placed his serviette by his plate and stood. "I understand. Dancing it is."

They danced, first the waltz, then a quadrille as best they could without other partners. By the end of the hour, she was breathless from exertion and longing.

Her fingers and thumb would not meet around his bulging arm. And that divot at the base of his neck had caused her to miss a step more than once when they were waltzing. She'd moved on from wanting to rest her fingertip there to wanting to suck it, having taken a page from his book from the prior evening.

Panting, she raised a hand at the end of the song. "Water, please."

"How about an ale?" he asked. "I bought a barrel from the pub in town."

"I've only ever had an ale once when I was young and stole my cousin's. Ladies—girls," she amended quickly, "are not encouraged to drink ale."

He snorted. "You must be joking. They quaffed it with the best of 'em in the pub back home."

Not having an answer, she shrugged.

"Come with me." He grabbed her hand, thanked the musicians, and tugged her down the hall to the kitchen. He'd set the barrel on two thick planks of wood running alongside it so it wouldn't roll off the counter. Now he grabbed two tankards and held them under the tap one at a time, passing her the first one.

Evie looked at the amount of beer in her cup warily. She enjoyed wine, but that was for sipping. She did not wish to lose her head around Xander, he was heady enough without alcohol in the mix.

Stepping to the kitchen door, he asked, "Shall we enjoy them by moonlight?"

"I'm not at all certain we'll see the moon behind the clouds, but I'd love a stroll through the gardens." Taking a tentative sip of her ale, Evie found it refreshing. It had an odd taste, perhaps from the way it fermented or the fact that it came from barley, but it wasn't bad. Just something to become accustomed to.

They strolled and sipped without speaking for a few minutes before he gestured at a stone bench.

She sank down with a sigh, and he settled beside her, sitting between her and the house. Backlit, he was all shadows and outlines, his massive shoulders blocking much of the light.

He set his tankard on the bench next to him and turned to face her, further darkening his features. "What is that look for?"

"It occurred to me—this morning, as I slept remarkably well last night—"

He barked a laugh.

"—that last night's fun was rather one-sided."

After a startled look that she'd reference their escapades of the previous night, he shook his head. "Not at all. That is why I thanked you. Seeing you come undone was the highlight of my entire time here."

She glanced down and sucked in a breath then looked him in the eyes. "Then I'll say it differently. I should like to have the opportunity to make you come undone. But as you might have guessed, I am unsure how to do that. Would you be so kind as to teach me?"

Her mother would have fainted dead away at her boldness, but Evie was proud of herself. On the other hand, her aunt would be clapping. Her mother had taught her to go after what she wanted but to work within society's confines. Her aunt had told her to ignore those limits. Either way, she wanted Xander.

Chapter Fifteen

Xander shifted on the bench, breathing hard. His hands wrapped around the front edge of the seat to stop himself from grabbing Evie and laying her out to pound her. If he thought too hard about what she wanted, he wouldn't need any help to explode in passion.

Plenty of pub patrons and even one or two of his employees had propositioned him, but Evie's genuine curiosity and interest in giving *him* pleasure, not using him for her own, was the most arousing thing he'd ever heard.

Swallowing, he tried again to be a gentleman—something he'd been before that term had been associated with his title. "'Tis unnecessary. And frankly, not wise."

She pouted; her expression was easy to read in the light shining out of the house windows over his shoulder. "That isn't fair."

He stifled a smile; he couldn't disagree. But his mother had raised him to respect women, no matter their station. "I know. But you must know life isn't fair. Aren't you the one teaching me how to protect the working people from the ogres of the aristocracy?"

Evie dropped her head.

"Besides, I doubt I could teach you for more than a minute before, er, coming undone."

Her face rose, a wicked grin on her lips. "Oh? I

should like to see that." She trailed fingers up his arm. "If you will na' show me, I shall have to guess. And perhaps do what I want, rather than what you might like. It can be an…experiment."

Her forefinger landed at the base of his throat, nestling there for a moment before she swept her hand up into his hair, gripping it to turn him toward the light. Releasing him momentarily, she scrambled up to kneel on the bench and reached for his shirt.

For someone who had seemed unfamiliar with kissing only days ago, she was a quick study and bold to boot. Dissuading her would be the right course of action, but her fearless approach had his blood surging away from his brain. Devilish thoughts shoved all gentlemanly teachings out of his head. He swallowed and remained still, somehow justifying this interlude by the fact that he wasn't initiating. Too, he daren't move for fear of clawing at her clothes as she was with his.

She tugged at his shirt, sliding it up and over his head. It floated to the ground in his peripheral vision as she sat back on her heels and stared. "Oh my."

He raised his brows then realized she could not see the implied question. "What?"

"You're so broad. Somehow bigger without clothes on, although one would expect them to add volume. And muscular. And slightly furry." Her hand petted his chest hair. "And warm."

A moan rumbled in his throat as her fingers left a trail of fire on his skin. His nipples had hardened even before she brushed over them. She came back to toy with them, and he couldn't contain his gasp.

"You like that. I suppose it makes sense. I certainly loved when you—" She leaned forward and licked, and he nearly came off the bench. "Mmm. A tad salty, perhaps from our dancing exertions, but delicious."

If she wanted salty, he could give her lots to taste. He gripped his cock through his clothing, unable to observe the niceties any longer. It was either grab himself in a woman's presence or make a mess of his trousers. As it was, his cock spurted pre-cum at her eager touch and words.

"I need more," Evie said, nearly undoing him further.

Hellfire, that was his favorite word on her lips. He rasped, "More what?"

"More skin." Her hands were already roaming his back, kneading his muscles as though testing them. She skimmed her hand across his waistline, teasing her finger between his trousers and his skin. He'd caught her ogling his bottom more than once and he guessed she wanted to touch him, just as he'd love to grip hers as he feasted on her again.

She asked, "Would you prefer to move inside? Last chance, or I am undressing you here."

He gulped. Of course, she'd never be able to undress him unless he allowed it, given their relative sizes, but having her warn him thus was almost his undoing. He didn't care about the rough surface or chill. Hell, he'd had sex in all sorts of strange places. The wine cellar of the pub, the stables, even over a keg once, although that last was his partner, not him. They'd had to check for splinters after.

Evie was done waiting. Shoving his shoulders to lean him back, she unbuttoned his falls and yanked at the trousers.

Afraid she would catch his cock in the fabric, he helped. Toeing off his low boots, he shucked his trousers and smallclothes, giving in to the inevitable. Just this once, he'd relax and enjoy. After all, he'd tried to do the right thing. The aggressive little maid wasn't having it.

In one swoop, she moved his tankard to the ground, laid him down, and straddled one of his legs, half kneeling, half standing over him to reach everything.

"Xander." Her whisper was full of awe. "You are amazing. Not beautiful; you're far too masculine for that word. Wondrous."

Her innocence beguiled him; it was easy to forget she'd likely never seen a naked man before. And—he glanced down—she could see all of him clearly now his shoulders weren't blocking the house lights. He needed to tread carefully here. Normally, he'd be guiding her head to his cock already. Instead, he laced his hands behind his head to allow her to go at her own pace.

She ran her hands over him, settling them on his chest. Leaning down, she followed the same path with her mouth.

The moisture from her lips caught the night air, and he shivered at the contrast of heat from her touch and cold from the breeze. His biceps bulged with the strain of not reaching for her.

That drew her attention, and she skimmed her teeth along his arm muscles, drawing a groan out of him.

Her hip came to rest on his cock, and her upper thigh nestled against his bollocks as she leaned closer.

"Do you know what happens between a man and a woman, Evie?" he managed to ask.

"I have an idea. My cousin filled in the blanks Mama wasn't comfortable sharing." She pulled back and gestured to where most of his blood seemed to be collecting. "That goes inside me, and your seed can cause a…delicate condition."

Despite her odd phrasing, the "your seed" made his cock jump and seep, and he blinked his eyes closed for a long moment before refocusing on her.

Blazes. She was staring at his member.

"Yes. And as you witnessed, it moves of its own accord sometimes as my pleasure builds. When I'm very aroused, my seed leaks out, both in eagerness and to help lubricate my path when I come inside you."

Gah, the pronouns, speaking as though the two of them were actually going to have intercourse, was going to make him blow his load straight up in the air.

He gritted out, "I wanted to warn you so you would not soil your dress."

She dragged her gaze away from his most eager part and cocked her head. "You're even thoughtful when you're in the midst of passion. You are the sweetest man."

That might kill his erection. He knew she meant well, but who wanted to be called sweet, especially at a moment such as this?

Chapter Sixteen

He really was the sweetest man, no matter that his mouth twisted in distaste when she said that. 'Twas no wonder her affections grew every day. All aspects of him appealed to her—intellect, brawn, and how he held her in high esteem, regardless of her position in life.

She reached out, then hesitated. "May I touch it?"

"Yes, please." His voice was hoarse.

She rather liked him begging. She wrapped her hand around his cock, shocked at how hot it was. No wonder it was swollen and red. Or perhaps it got hot because it swelled? No matter, she'd investigate that next time.

Right now, finding his favorite spots was what she wanted most. He'd seemed to know hers without help the previous night. "What feels best?"

His eyes were closed when she flicked a glance up at him, his mouth slack. "All of it. Any of it. Perhaps next time I can be more specific. Right now, I'm overcome." Her fingers slid up and over the edge of the mushroom head, and he groaned.

"Ah ha." She circled her fingers around him right below that lip of skin and glided them up and down in small movements.

"Evie, ah gads."

She stopped. "I don't want to end this too soon. You toyed with me last night, and I'm not done exploring here."

His hips lowered from where he'd raised them toward her, and he sagged against the bench. She hadn't even noticed.

Bringing her other hand to the pouch below the steel rod she held, she cupped it gently.

"Ah, yes." His cock leaped in her hand and she nearly released it. It oozed more liquid.

"Evie, if you keep this up, I'll come. A fountain of it." He moved his arms to grip the sides of the bench above his hips and his knuckles were white with strain.

An idea formed.

He stared at her through bleary eyes.

She smirked. "Based on last night, and conversations belowstairs, and your concern for my apparel, it seems best that I find a way to avoid a mess."

With that, she leaned down and licked him.

He shouted an unintelligible curse.

She barely noticed. He was salty and thick and unlike anything she'd ever tasted. More, she wanted his cock to leap in her mouth, wanted to run her tongue around that domed head, wanted to swallow against him and feel him enter her in a way different and yet similar to the night before. Sealing her lips around his head, she pressed her tongue against the edge of the helmet and sucked.

"Evie!" he whisper-shouted. His hands had come up to hover over her hair.

She slipped him out, still holding him at her lips, and smiled. "You can touch me."

"No, you don't understand. If I do, I'll want to pull your head until your nose is pressed against me, unable to breathe, wanting to gag."

"Really? That's what you like?" She tilted her head.

His hips kept jerking through her grip in tiny

movements as though unable to remain still. He nodded.

"I'm willing to try. Touch me as you'd like." And with that, she sank her mouth onto him, sliding him in as far as she could. When the back of her throat stopped his progress, she kept pushing and angling, trying to figure out how to make it work.

When she came up for breath, frustrated, he said, "Evie, what you were doing before was fantastic. I never dreamed I'd have your mouth on me at all. You don't need to—ahh."

She'd swallowed him down again, ignoring his mutterings. Finally, his hand came to push his length down, changing the angle in her mouth and throat, and oh, there it went.

It cut off her air, so she slid up, took a deep breath, and slid back down again.

"Evie, Evie," he said urgently, his hands tugging at her. "You'll get more than you bargained for if you do that again."

He has no idea what I bargained for. He'd done the same for her last night, finishing her until his face was wet. She wanted their exchange to be fair and equally pleasurable.

Fair in this, perhaps, but you're lying to him. How fair is that?

Shutting away such extraneous thoughts, she raised her head, took a deep breath, and sucked him as deep as she could.

Under her, his hips continued to jerk, and his fingers threaded through her hair. "Yes, Evie, yes. Drink it all, then."

His cock pulsed in her mouth, rippling, nearly making her gag, followed by hot liquid spurting down her throat in blast after blast. So this was how his orgasms felt. She liked it a lot. There was power in having her mouth on him, his essence pouring into her, knowing she'd caused that. She was unbearably aroused, but strangely sated. As he had said the night before, this was all the satisfaction she needed for the night. There would be other times for mutual exploration.

And throughout, he'd been so careful with her once again. This man would make a fantastic husband.

She was almost positive she was in love with him, but she wanted a bit more time to explore that and all of this new world of sensuality. Aunt Lou would be able to help her find the courage to reveal her identity. She hoped.

Chapter Seventeen

Xander needed a moment to recover after Evie released him. Her cheek rested against his abdomen, and she nuzzled into his stomach while he stroked her hair. Taking a deep breath, he attempted to collect his wits. This woman would be his undoing.

"Hellfire, that was the most intense bit of tipping the velvet I've ever experienced."

"I enjoyed it as well, my lo—Rutla—Xander. I suppose we've achieved a sufficient level of familiarity for first names." She chuckled.

He laughed. She apparently didn't realize that she'd called his first name in the throes of passion on more than one occasion already.

They sat up, and he redressed. Tugging her close, he leaned in to kiss her.

She threw a hand up, covering her mouth. "Oh, I, ah…"

"Come, now, the least I can do is kiss you in thanks after what you were kissing for me."

"Well, when you put it like that." She leaned up for a leisurely kiss.

His bed was huge; perhaps he could keep her with him all night. But no, he wasn't ready to tarnish her innocence any more than he already had. He needed to take things slow. He walked her inside and upstairs in silence, consumed by his thoughts. But when they reached the floor with his bedroom, she placed a hand on his chest and shook her head.

"I'll walk you to your room," he replied to her hesitation.

"And what happens if another of the staff is up and about and sees you?"

"Oh."

"Quite. I'm fine, but thank you for the chivalry." She gentled her refusal with a smile and a squeeze of his hand before leaving him to ascend the stairs to the servants quarters.

Xander was left to lay staring at the ceiling plaster for the rest of the night, wondering why he felt so trapped when a dukedom was supposed to bring as much freedom as a man could wish for.

He needed some time to think, and he did his best thinking while "working" as he had his whole adult life. After informing the staff that he'd be in the village at the pub most of the day, he set out. Banks wasn't there when he arrived, so he chatted with the driver of the cart delivering Scotch. Dressed to work, he introduced himself only as Xander, and the man was none the wiser to his annoying title.

When Banks arrived, he put Xander to work, shaking his head and muttering about dukes who didn't appreciate what they had the whole while.

Xander grinned and said, "You're quite welcome for the free labor."

Unloading barrels of ale from the next delivery and dragging them down into the cellar resulted in having to rearrange the existing barrels so the oldest were used first. Working in the dimly lit dank cellar gave him the perfect opportunity to turn his focus inward, as the manual labor was second nature and did not require mental acuity.

Despite Evie's sneaking into the library that one night, Xander was fairly sure he trusted her more than he trusted some pre-arranged Ton chit on a marriage contract. She'd helped him in so many ways already, as though she genuinely wanted him to succeed in his duties. Plus, she could set his trousers on fire with a mere look.

If he'd still been a pub manager, his path would be clear. He could court her, maybe even tup her, and decide later to marry her. But now, as a duke, he needed heirs, so marriage was mandatory. Of course, they could carry on an affair, but if he had to wed anyway, why not the person of his choosing? He'd have to entertain in London, and people would expect him to choose someone with a pedigree, but they'd already be questioning his, so there'd be no winning there either way.

In order to show her he was serious about marrying her, he'd need to have restraint. There was no doubt in his mind that she'd never been with a man before. If he tupped her now, the difference in their stations might make her feel as though she was forced to wed him. He wanted to show her in every way that he saw her as an equal.

As soon as he returned to the monstrosity that was now his home, he'd jot a note to the Duke of Cranbrook requesting a visit. After all, wasn't that what they were offering with this Wayward Dukes Alliance—help with sticky situations? His thoughts continued to circle on the path forward, and he considered riding to Cranbrook, but he didn't know the etiquette for inviting one's self to a duke's home or, worse, showing up uninvited.

Exhausted from his mental gymnastics as much as the manual labor, he headed upstairs and requested a slice of steak and kidney pie and an ale.

Banks joined him as the pub was quiet mid-afternoon between the midday meal and the evening revelry.

Given his history, Xander was curious about the owner. "Do you make all the managerial decisions here? How involved is the owner?"

Banks looked startled, then snorted a laugh. "Until recently, the owner was quite passive. I gave him monthly reports, but he didn't care to be part of the day-to-day operations or decisions."

"That must have been nice. Is he interfering more now, then?"

"I wouldn't say interfering. Just more hands on. Helpful, even." The pub manager struggled to get the words out through chuckles.

"What's funny? Who is this nob anyway?"

Banks bent over the table, guffawing before he straightened. "Finally, the right question. You are, my lord. You own this place. I thought you knew."

Abashed, Xander hung his head. "I haven't gotten that far in reviewing my holdings. I beg your pardon. Is that why you allowed me to help? Because you didn't think you could refuse?"

"Nah, I sort of wanted to see how a duke handled kegs and the like. I think a part of me was waiting to see you fail, so I could feel superior. Instead, here we are, quaffing ale together."

"I'm grateful, either way. And quite glad to prove you wrong, besides," Xander said with a grin.

With new purpose, he rode back to his oversized

home. Here was a situation he could remedy, a place where he could directly improve someone's life who worked hard every day. For the first time, he relaxed and enjoyed the pretty road through his estate, although he still shook his head at the sprawling manor home.

Never more grateful for staff, he tossed the reins to a groom, kicked the dirt off his boots as best he could, and aimed for the library. Another first—the prospect of paperwork didn't bring frustration.

On a shelf behind his desk sat a long line of binders holding reports, sorted by property. Prior years' reports were stored in the attic. He'd gotten three-quarters of the way through them, having asked Munroe to prioritize them by size and complexity to ensure things ran smoothly for the people working in each business. As he hadn't seen the pub yet, that meant it ran smoothly and was not a great impact on his holdings. Which meant it was something he could do without. On the other hand, it was Banks's world.

He focused on the last dozen. None bore the name of the public house, but one stated, "Rutland." With his luck, he owned half the town. He pulled the volume from the shelf and dropped it on his desk with a thud.

Inside, the list of holdings wasn't quite half the town but sure enough included the pub. Xander flipped through several months' reports from Banks. It did quite well. The manager had expanded his offerings of whisky to include an Irish one after taxes on those imports were recently reduced. Well-cooked fare and the resulting competition between that and the Scotches from their northern neighbors drew a regular crowd.

Xander propped his chin on his fists and stared down at the reports. If only he knew how to execute this particular plan. He recalled someone—he wasn't sure if it had been Lancaster, Hollibrook, or Munroe—mentioning deeds for ownership but had no idea where he'd find such a thing or if it was in Rutland. Lancaster might be the keeper of such things.

He rang the bell for a servant. Too impatient to wait, he stood and stomped toward the door, nearly colliding with Rogers as the man opened the door.

"Rogers, there you are. By the by, what is your first name, man?"

"George, sir, but I prefer Rogers, if it pleases you."

"Ah, all right."

"You rang, Your Grace?" the servant asked mildly.

"Is Munroe still here?"

"I don't believe so. I understood that you dismissed him this morning before your outing." Rogers' brows were nearly at his hairline.

"Right, right. But dammit, I need his help."

"Is there someone else who might help you?" Rogers said and cleared his throat.

"No. Even Munroe cannot half the time." Xander stomped back to his desk, picked up the portfolio with the pub's reports, and slammed it down.

Rogers started, took a giant step backwards into the hallway, and closed the door.

Xander hadn't seen Evie. Usually she was somewhere on the ground floor working until their sessions. He strode back to the door. "Where is Evie?"

Rogers' eyes were wide as he stuttered, "She-she took a half day. I think she has a-a relative nearby?"

Xander refrained from growling at the footman and said only, "Have her see me when she returns."

Damnation, another plan on hold until he got help.

Chapter Eighteen

"Aunt Lou," Evie sang as she knocked a second time on her aunt's front door before opening it and letting herself in.

"Aunt Lou? Are you awake? Anyone?" Her aunt only had two part-time staff, choosing to lead a simple life.

Evie walked to the kitchen at the rear of the house. Louisa was usually up and about by now, despite it being quite early by London Ton standards.

Seeing a dirty teacup by the sink gave Evie hope she wasn't waking her aunt. Peeking out the kitchen door, there was no sign of her aunt in the garden. It seemed too early to be out and about, but Evie daren't look for her around town for fear of exposure of her disguise.

She sat at her aunt's writing desk in the small parlor and pulled out foolscap and pen and ink. Unable to fathom how to summarize everything that had gone on, she started at random.

Dear Aunt Lou,

Never let it be said I'm lazy. This job is hard work. But it's honest work, and the duke is more than fair to his staff. I shall pester Mother to give the servants a pay increase when I get home.

I've managed to spend some time with X— the duke (how that came about is a story for in person), and he is

more than I hoped for.
    I need—

Voices and footsteps came from above and Evie started, ink splattering across the page. Damnation! Aunt Lou had a guest. A male guest, no less.

Evie's muscles loosened, and her mouth curled up in a smile. Nicely done, Auntie.

A man's voice, closer to the stairs, said, "Lulu, I must go. I'm late."

"Thank you for the tea. You know I'd rather have had—"

"I know what you'd rather have had, minx." They both laughed.

Evie barely managed to stifle a shriek of laughter herself. Her aunt, a minx. However, there were more pressing matters. Her aunt would tell her of her latest amour when she was ready. So Evie needed to get out of the house before being seen.

Dropping the pen and capping the ink, she left everything as it was. Aunt Lou would understand and hopefully see it before the nib of the pen was ruined from dried ink.

The work boots lingering on the second stair down paused. Evie scrambled out the nearby front door and closed the portal shut with a gentle click to hurry away.

As she tromped through town toward the duke's home, she could not recall where she'd left off in her note. Hopefully, she'd written enough that her aunt would understand. She needed more time with Xander in this lovely bubble hidden away from London and society.

When they'd made this plan, they expected Evie was

unlikely to have a way to correspond with Lou. So they decided on a month to live in the duke's household to evaluate his suitability. At that point, Louisa would write to her family and request that they join them, noting that the duke was in residence and it might be a good time to discuss the marriage contract.

Her month was up in only a few days, and Evie wasn't ready. Oh, she'd made her decision, but further assurance that Xander cared enough to overlook her spying and follow through on the betrothal was needed.

Following the dirt road out of town, her mind wouldn't focus on plans. Instead, scenes of Xander laid out before her like a feast flooded her vision. The prior evening's activities played on repeat, and it was all she could do to walk a straight line.

That was it. She'd been thinking like Evie, Xander's maid and erstwhile friend, whereas the solution lay in her true identity, a member of the Ton. As a lady, she was already compromised if her charade came to light, so she may as well enjoy the rewards. Xander needed to teach her more and to thoroughly debauch her, and she couldn't wait.

Chapter Nineteen

Xander had not arranged for musicians this evening. In addition to being tired from the physical work at the pub, he was behind on paperwork. Hellfire, he detested all the correspondence more than anything. More than any of that, though, he needed to talk to Evie about deeds of ownership. He wasn't sure he wanted to share the details of his plan yet, but hoped she had some information for him rather than waiting on correspondence to Lancaster the solicitor, all the way down in London.

He turned into the dining room and stopped short.

Evie's hair was one of his favorite aspects of her beauty, but her maid's cap usually hid it. Normally, she only removed the blasted cap at his request. Tonight, she'd taken the initiative. More, she'd left her hair down, pinned back from her face and resting on the upper swells of her breasts in shiny waves.

His breath caught in his throat. He pictured her in a lady's gown, all fancy fabric and lower cut bodice than her serviceable maid's dress. Satin undergarments would complement her delicate, smooth skin. Perhaps he'd indulge in buying her stays and chemises to match each dress. Either way, he had every intention of seeing her there as his duchess.

He strode to his chair. Enough talk about undergarments or the footmen in the room would know his thoughts given the cut of his trousers.

"Evie, you look lovely. Thank you for wearing your hair down."

Tilting her head, she tucked her hair behind an ear and gave a small smile.

"I'm afraid I must keep our meal short, and forsake dancing this evening," he said as their wine was poured and soup bowls were placed before them.

Her lips pursed in a moue of disappointment, and Xander had to fiddle with his serviette on his lap to disguise the need to rearrange his hardening cock for comfort. She said, "May I ask why?"

Because otherwise I may lay you across this table and suckle every inch of you, and my plan to keep you requires I have some modicum of decorum.

"I was out much of yesterday and today and am terribly behind on sorting through the duke's—ahem, my—correspondence. And more arrives every day." He was shaking his head by the time he finished the thought. If anything was going to take him out of the mood to ravish her, that stack of mail would.

"I understand. That is perhaps a mite more pressing than learning the waltz, I suppose." Her tone was wistful.

He cast her a questioning glance with an arched brow.

"I enjoy dancing with you, Rutland. 'Tis certainly more fun than polishing the furniture." She shrugged one shoulder and grinned.

Somewhere nearby, Duncan the footman coughed.

Xander laughed, "I understand."

"How was your day out?" she asked as the soups were removed and the main course placed before them.

"Lovely." His out-of-practice muscles ached, but

nothing beat hauling barrels for keeping fit. "I was down at the pub for much of it."

"Do you conduct business there?"

"You could say that." Xander slid a glance at the footman. The intention was never to keep his 'hobby' a secret. Chances were that Banks had already passed the gossip of him working at the pub in town. But it also wouldn't do to get too familiar with the servants. While treating everyone with respect was imperative, he never got too close to pub staff in the past after that one regrettable incident with the barmaid. Distance as an employer seemed better. He'd share his pastime with Evie in private. He was willing to bet she'd understand and perhaps appreciate it.

"I hope it was productive, then." She looked a little disappointed he hadn't shared more details.

"What of your day? Polish much furniture?" he asked with a grin.

Duncan stifled another snort.

"Actually, I had the morning off, the first time since I arrived. I thought it was good timing when I received your note that we weren't meeting regarding Parliamentary documents and went to the village to visit."

"I'm glad. Everyone here works quite hard. I need to speak to Mrs. Betters about the staff's work schedule."

Evie and Duncan both stared at him with raised brows.

"What?"

"Dukes rarely care about staff holidays or work schedules. And even in the more generous households, the lady of the house typically manages that."

"Well, I don't have one of those, do I? And whilst I

know you're used to London, where Parliamentary Acts are more prominent in conversation, this place is quite removed. I believe it is in my best interests to prioritize the world I can most affect just as much as the greater one out there where I am but one vote of many."

Evie nodded. "I respect that. I'd never quite thought of it that way. And at some point, you'll wed, and then your duchess will help you on both counts, which will ease the burden some."

If she only knew my plan.

He stood, waving off pudding as it came out. He wanted to read more about his holdings before he asked her questions. "Please, share it in the kitchen. I need to get to work."

* * * *

Two hours later, he was ready to tear his hair out at the roots. Standing, he stretched his arms up and out and arched his back to counter having hunched over papers since the evening meal. Even with a candelabra on each side of him, his eyes were straining.

He strolled to the sideboard and poured a whisky. One of the absolute best benefits of being a duke, beside his gorgeous and helpful maid and a bed that finally fit him, was always having excellent whisky on hand. As a pub manager, he'd sampled all sorts, balancing the budget versus what would sell with variety and quality. Most patrons in his brother's pub drank beer. Only the souses and the most discerning, like his stepfather the Earl of Northumberland, ventured in to drink the finer spirits. So he'd stocked basic rotgut and the nicest Scotch the pub's finances allowed for.

The house had a selection of Scotch and Irish

Whiskey, although duties on both were threatening to increase their prices further. Depending on his mood, he sampled one or the other. Tonight, his mood leaned to the mellow. Also, frustrated arousal without an outlet. But more mellow because he was playing the long game. So Irish Whiskey it was.

Rolling the second sip around on his tongue, he meandered back to the desk to stare down at the unending piles of paper, wishing he could trust himself enough to have Evie help him. Although her days were long enough that he should not keep her up at night.

A rustle of skirts caught his attention. She stood at the entrance of the library as though he'd conjured her, still wearing that sack of a uniform. His brows quirked. "I thought you'd be long abed."

"I was waiting for you to call for me. Usually, I help you with this if Munroe isn't here, and we missed our afternoon session." She gestured to the desk.

"I'd hoped to get through more without help. 'Tis been nearly a month."

She shook her head. "Do not get discouraged. Not being in London, at White's or Brook's or one of the gentlemen's clubs, talking about this, you'll have to read through each one. Those men find others whose opinions they trust and share the burden. Plus, 'tis all a bit out of context for you, I suspect."

He nodded, taking another sip. She peered at his tumbler, and he tilted it toward her. "Care for some?"

Taking his glass, she sniffed the amber liquid and raised it to her lips, barely wetting them before pulling the glass away and licking them.

He nearly groaned, instead choosing to take a gulp of whiskey.

She hummed, tilting her head.

"Do you like it? Would you like your own glass?" he asked.

"I think I'd like it better this way," she answered, leaning in to lick his lips, twisting them open to slide her tongue against his, humming again low in her throat.

He clinked the glass down on the desk and grabbed her, slanting his lips across hers and sliding a hand through her hair to the base of her neck.

"Delicious," she muttered against him.

Her hand came to brand his chest with its heat. The other was smoothing down his spine to where his shirt disappeared in his trousers. He felt a tug, then her palm slid over the long muscles of his back, skin-to-skin. She arched into him with a groan that echoed in his chest.

"Perhaps I need to sample whiskey off other parts of you, to see which I like best," she muttered as both hands tugged his shirt upwards.

His cock surged, and for a moment, he allowed himself to envision her sucking whiskey off it. But his plans took priority. "Evie, I don't want to take advantage of you."

She drew back with a slight frown. "I was offering. How is that taking advantage?"

"Of our positions then."

"This," she said, gesturing between them then fitting her fingers around the iron rod poking her lower belly, "has never been about our positions."

He groaned before summoning words to try again. "I want to show you the proper respect."

"And you are," she murmured, her hands once again roaming under his shirt. "You're giving me fair access."

He grabbed her wrists to hold her still.

Frowning more, she looked up at him. "What is this about? What changed from last night? And the last time we were in this room at night?"

He gulped. He wasn't ready to reveal his plan until the Wayward Dukes gave their advice. "Nothing. I—I'm only trying to do the right thing. That marriage contract says I am not at liberty to woo anyone else."

It was a lie, but the pretty maid wouldn't know that.

An undecipherable look crossed her face before she smoothed her expression. Stepping back, she tugged her hands out of his hold. "Who's talking about wooing? This was all straightforward until tonight. I helped you because you needed it, not because I worked for you. Likewise, you taught me a few aspects of pleasure because you were attracted to me and I wanted it, not because you had power over me."

He nodded, chagrined. "You are correct. Because of all that, I have come to care for you. I became concerned that I was taking advantage of the situation. All this is still so new to me. I don't understand its limits."

Evie stepped toward him. "I shall tell you my limits. And I know you will respect them. You needn't worry."

Her hair shone in the candlelight, her lush lips begged for his, and her breath smelled of his favorite spirits. His conscience could no longer fight her and his desire. He'd find a way to toe the line between pleasure and honor. After all, they'd both experienced orgasms without her innocence being compromised. And if his plan worked, she'd be his wife in short order, so they could continue to explore alternative paths now, and soon, soon, they could ignite the full conflagration of pleasure between them. If his idea didn't... Well, if it didn't, he could not see himself marrying anyone else, so he'd make it right with her. He wanted her by his side, no matter what.

He stepped in. "Let's take the decanter to my bedroom and be comfortable."

Her eyes flared. "Yes, please."

He grinned.

Chapter Twenty

Eight nights later, Evie was frustrated. Sexually and mentally. She'd spent every one of those nights in Xander's bed. She'd had plenty of orgasms, a plethora of pleasure, but he hadn't been willing to consummate their intimacy with intercourse. More than once, they'd argued about it, and each time, he'd wooed her into silence with caresses, finding all her most sensitive spots.

This evening, he'd begun with his fingers again. With her spreadeagled on the bed and him lying propped on an elbow alongside, he'd found a spot just inside her that was almost painful at first. He'd started with slow, gentle glides, adding his thumb to press her nub just above where his finger entered her.

When he withdrew and slid down the bed, she'd pouted, thinking he was leaving. But then he wedged his massive shoulders between her knees and licked up her center. A short scream escaped as she nearly shot off the bed. Despite having performed a similar act for him, she'd never considered he'd want to do the same. His mouth created a different yet equally delicious pleasure as his hand.

He grinned up at her wide-eyed stare before suckling her flesh into his mouth. Thrusting his fingers back in to find that magical spot, he tongued her and pistoned, somehow knowing when she was ready for a faster, harder stroke.

When he sped up, pleasure spiked so fast it bordered on pain. She'd stiffened and gripped his hair with a whispered shriek, "Xander!"

"Shh, let it happen. You know I will keep you safe."

"Oh! Oh!" Her stomach muscles kept tightening, her hands now clenching and unclenching on the bedclothes. Her hips thrust up without conscious thought, then dropped for a second between his strokes, only to spear the air on his next finger curl. Sweat broke out in her armpits and along her hairline. She stared at Xander with her mouth open, unable to voice her request that he slow down, unsure she wanted him to.

His face went fuzzy as ecstasy struck like lightning, twisting her on the sheets with sharp, hot talons.

He slowed, allowing the storm to recede.

Evie blinked, her hands and legs lying limp at her sides. "My word, that was intense."

One side of his mouth tipped up in a half-smile.

He deserved the self-satisfaction of a job well done. Now she had another approach to add to her repertoire. Perhaps she could push him to complete her knowledge.

"My turn." She rose and shoved his shoulder to get him flat on his back. Straddling him, she licked her favorite spots—the skin under his ear, his nipples, along his hip bone—before taking his shaft in her mouth and repeating the rhythm he'd used on her.

He stopped her before he reached climax, however. Instead, he'd flipped them again, so she was on her back. Kneeling between her legs, he'd drawn her thighs on top of his.

For a second, she'd hoped he'd given in, and she'd enjoy the full experience of making love with this hard-working man turned duke. Because it was love.

Everything he did had erased any doubts she may have harbored. She hadn't needed the time she'd requested from her aunt. He was more than she could have hoped for in a husband, a future father to her children, and a representative of fairness in the House of Lords. She wanted nothing more than to spend her days with him in the library and her nights with him like this.

But her wish was not to be. Instead, he'd tugged her hips closer, taken his cock in hand, and rubbed it along her folds. Her orgasm ensured that her swollen flesh was wet with her residual excitement. His cock was covered in her saliva and was weeping pre-ejaculate besides.

"Hold yourself open," he commanded.

When she did, he aimed for the hard kernel of nerves already building to another climax. His hips thrust as she imagined they would if he were inside her, but instead, the length of him slid forward and back, igniting sensations that radiated through her. His free hand came to pinch her nipple, and she arched her back toward him in response.

Grabbing his thighs, she levered herself in counterpoint, meeting his forward drives, speeding his reversals.

"Can you come from this?" he asked.

An unfamiliar warmth went through her at the question, emotional rather than physical. Even in the throes of passion after she'd climaxed and he hadn't, he was considerate.

She nodded.

"Then hurry."

His comment made her smile until he brought his free hand below his cock to slide into her weeping channel.

She raised her hips and pumped them in a tight, fast rhythm under the head of his cock where he was most sensitive, one hand holding him against her at the right angle for them both.

"Yes, yes, that," he gritted out.

Pleasure spiraled through her again, and she pulsed against his cock, squeezing him with her hand for a long moment before collapsing flat.

He gripped his shaft and shunted his hand up and down it a few quick rounds before spurting onto her belly in long strands of thick white liquid.

After cleaning them both with a cloth from the washstand, he lay beside her again.

They'd taken to sharing tidbits of their childhoods with each other—Evie's were suitably edited not to reveal her privilege—after sex.

"'Tis your turn, I believe," she said.

"Did I ever tell you about my time in London?"

* * * *

Ohh, this sounded interesting. She'd asked questions about his work at the Old Shoreston pub but had not discovered his reasons for disliking the nobility. Indeed, his comments about his mother's new husband, the Earl of Northumberland, were complimentary. Perhaps this would shed some light on his feelings. "No."

"This is not really from my childhood, mind you. I was down there working to help my stepbrother a few years ago."

"Your stepbrother?"

"Luke Lynwood, heir to my stepfather from a previous marriage. As opposed to my half-brother, Bruce, who I grew up with and who owns the pub I managed."

She nodded her understanding, combing her fingers through the light covering of hair on his chest.

"He was setting up a place—I guess you'd say a cross between a hospital and an inn—for men to recover from a dependency on spirits, snuff, or gaming. It's called Free Your Spirits."

"Really?" she asked with a smile at the name. Her fingers paused. 'Twas lovely to hear of a titled person having empathy for those who struggled, especially a man. Too many did not.

"He had had help—from the woman he later married—with his own recovery and wanted to do the same for others. So I was helping get the remaining rooms cleaned and furnished as the first guests moved in. I'm sure you won't be surprised to hear there were lots of candidates for the program."

"Hmm. You are correct, I'm not surprised, although I suspect there were plenty who weren't interested in pursuing sobriety, too."

"Possibly. I wasn't involved in that part. But I *was* pressed into servitude." He shuddered anew at the memory. "I have never seen the like. Grown men crying, vomiting, pissing themselves, and expecting others to coddle them and clean up after them. They acted like spoiled brats."

Unfortunately, it didn't shock her because she had encountered many an entitled nobleman. She nodded.

"I've been in the wrong place at the wrong time at the pub. I'm not a stranger to piss and puke. But even the drunkest of drunks apologizes, especially if I'm trying to help them. Instead, these blokes spat out commands as to what I could do to serve them after cleaning up their mess or complained of the smell as though I was taking too long. One sat in a corner and cried for his mother."

She almost laughed at the look of distaste he made as he said the last part.

"I don't know how Luke does it. I nearly threw a punch more than once. At one point, a bloke started to cast up his accounts while lying down. I rolled him to the floor so he wouldn't choke. The nob tried to get me fired for being rough with him." He shook his head, still pissed on behalf of any working man whose word might be tested against a nob's. "What if I hadn't been a relation? Would Luke have believed me then? I wonder. As it is, I feel lucky; we hadn't known each other that long."

"He sounds like a nice man," she ventured.

"He is, and he has the patience of a saint with those whiners. The last straw was when I walked into a pub near his home, where I was a guest. I saw one man who had cried and tried to punch me as I helped him into bed, standing there with a drink in his hand again. When I said something to him, he looked down his nose at me and asked how I thought that *my betters'* behavior could be any of my business." Xander threw a hand up in exacerbation and barked a bitter laugh. "He honestly thought he was better than me."

"Seems a dangerous thing to say in such a public place. You could have referenced his terrible behavior from his time at Luke's."

"No, you don't understand. That is the beauty and the ugliness of the Ton. Luke lives in a fancy part of London. So the pub was full of this nob's cronies and peers. They'd have believed him over me, and indeed none of them wanted me in the establishment to start with. 'Twas a damned pub—by definition, a public house. I had less exposure to their wives, but from what little I saw, they didn't seem to have an original thought in their head, doing what their husbands told them. Even when their spouses were drunkards." His voice rose with impassioned bitterness. Throwing out a hand, he finished with, "These are the 'lords' I'm supposed to sit next to in the House of Lords, and the 'ladies' I should invite into my home and worry about their opinions of where Bruce sits at my table. 'Tis as ridiculous as it is annoying."

Xander's expression was so twisted with disdain, Evie cringed thinking of what his reaction would be to finding out she was one of those nobs. Despite her certainty that she loved him, she was glad she'd told her aunt she needed more time before Louisa should write to her parents.

Chapter Twenty-One

Xander stood at the window staring out at the morning light. He still couldn't quite believe he'd told her about London. Just saying the words again had brought back a rush of humiliation and anger. The same feelings he experienced every time thoughts of titled nobles entered his brain. Yet, irony of ironies, here he was, a duke.

Walking back to sit at his desk, he again performed a rough calculation of when he could expect Cranbrook. Normally, living on the north edge of England had many advantages. Namely few visitors from outside the region, and even fewer from London. However, frustration at the time it took to travel anywhere or even send correspondence ate at him. Waiting for the Wayward Dukes Alliance to receive his missive and arrive was agony. He picked up his pen, but after a few taps that scattered ink across the documents in front of him, he threw it down and leaned back, looking out the library window once again.

Evie did not seem overly concerned with the inequities in their status, but he was. She should feel like an equal in all aspects of their relationship. The betrothal contract request did not feel real, but it bothered him almost as much as his title versus her employment did. It was one more puzzle he had to solve before he could marry the woman he chose. The one who was patient with him, who laughed with him, and who gave everything of herself to him. He needed Evie in his life forever. London and Lords could go hang. They could do what they wished up here, and no one would care that she'd once been a maid and he'd once been a barkeeper.

However, until he knew what it would take to politely decline the damned betrothal request, silence had to prevail so she wouldn't be hurt. Every night as they stripped to their skin and were intimate in almost every way two people could be, he bit his tongue. The words "I love you" were in his mouth, gaze, and every caress. Hopefully, she saw what he couldn't say.

In addition, he was eager to empower Banks to thank him for his unwavering acceptance and support as the man ran a business that Xander owned.

Bringing up London and Luke reminded him of his stepfather. The Earl of Northumberland hadn't worried about marrying a commoner when Xander's mother became his wife. Of course, that was a second marriage after his heir came of age, so the Ton might be more forgiving. North, however, did not care whether or not they forgave him; he did what he wanted.

Xander jotted a note to his mother and North, telling them he was thinking of a visit, and put it in the pile to be posted.

Evie entered, singing out, "Good morning."

Her voice reminded him of his questions about her speech. "Evie, come have tea before you begin your duties."

"Whatever you desire, my lord." She winked at him.

He would not be distracted, however much that phrase made him want to put her on her knees under his desk to serve him from there all day. "You told me you grew up in London. But your elocution and choice of words are quite different than any of the blokes I met there. How is that?"

Her face shuttered, her gaze going to her lap for a moment before she inhaled and re-engaged. "I think people learn much of their speech and expressions from their parents. Mine were careful to keep me from slang or other regional jargon. And of course the household I spent time in most recently was quite refined."

"I see." He'd picked up some vernacular from the pub that he hadn't learned at home, so he understood. "Thank you."

"Why did you ask? Do I talk funny?" she asked with a nervous expression.

"No, not at all. But nor do you sound like anyone local or most of the people I encountered in London."

She took a last sip of tea and stood. "Well, then. I should get back to polishing chair legs. Unless there's something else you'd like me to polish?"

He shook his head, chuckling. "Get to work with you. I'm amazed I can get anything done around here with you tempting me. Next thing I know, you'll be wiggling those delicious buttocks at me as you work."

She did exactly that until it was time to work through more correspondence together.

Chapter Twenty-Two

They supped together that night as they did most nights in the past sennight, without even attempting to pretend it was to teach him the formalities of entertaining.

The next morning, Mrs. Betters assigned her to dust the artwork on the walls of the entryway. She was wielding her duster on a stick along the top of a frame, leaning over a side table, when horses clattered in the drive. Her heart pounded, fearing exposure. Or perhaps worse, something that would pull Xander to London without having found a way to confess her true identity.

With Rogers right there, she could not duck into the front parlor to identify the riders. Stuck, she focused on dusting without pulling the frame off the wall as the footman answered the door.

A man said, "I believe His Grace is expecting us."

He said more, but Evie's ears buzzed with fear. She recognized that voice. 'Twas the Marquess of Hollibrook back for a second visit, this time with a younger duke she knew only in passing. She lowered her gaze and realized she was in front of a mirror rather than a painting.

Glancing at the men waiting for the footman to go find the duke to announce them, her gaze met the marquess's as he stared at her. He tilted his head, frowning, and took a half step toward her.

Gulping, she tugged her cap lower on her forehead

and raised her arm to hide her reflection. The footman returned, saving her. "His Grace will see you in his library. This way, gentlemen."

A breath of relief escaped out her mouth. He wouldn't look for a distant relative to be a maid, especially when he knew her family was flush. Hopefully, he did not recall that her aunt lived here.

Her hopes were dashed when, after the footman had disappeared down the hall to request tea service, Hollibrook stepped out of the library door and pulled it closed behind him.

She stared unblinking as he strode toward her.

"Evie." His voice held wonder. "It *is* you. Why are you dressed thus?"

"My lord." She curtsied as her heart threatened to pound out of her chest.

His gaze narrowed. "If I recall, you were betrothed to the former duke. I was excited to have family nearby again, as was my father. What are you about, Evie?"

"Shh." She looked around him for Rogers's return, then scampered into the front parlor, gesturing for him to follow.

"My father sent a note requesting that Xa"—she corrected herself at his censorious look—"His Grace honor the previous betrothal without asking me or any of us having met the man."

"Then why not invite him to London? Or have the family pay a visit? Or anything rather than masquerading as a maid in his household?" He turned his hands up and shook his head.

"Surely, you understand that women have little to no say in these things, and I desired to know what he was like before he—and I—decided if we wanted the marriage contract honored in light of the previous duke's unfortunate demise." Her hands twisted in her apron. Realizing that, she shook them out and fisted them at her sides.

"That doesn't explain spying on him like this." The marquess frowned. "Wait, did your mother's sister have anything to do with this?"

She shook her head, declining to answer that. "I know your politics are more in line with mine than with my father's. Only after the betrothal did I discover that the previous duke's were closer to my father's. I was young and silly when he asked for my hand, and now…I am not."

Hollibrook grimaced and waved one hand up and down her length. "I would argue that you are, given this getup."

"What would you have had me do?"

"Visit with your family like a proper young lady."

She caught herself before she stamped her foot. Men couldn't understand. But she had to try to explain it to her second cousin so he wouldn't betray her confidence to Xander. "You know we'd be supervised every minute. Besides, you met him. If we'd visited before now, Xander had only just come into his title. He would not have been ready to consider marriage."

"Ignoring the fact that there are good reasons for such supervision, whether or not he is ready, 'tis time." His mouth set in a grim line, the marquess turned toward the door.

"No, please! I need to be the one to tell him. 'Tis just—I need a bit more time to determine how to do that."

"You have two days. You will tell him before we

leave, or I shall.”

"Yes, my lord.” She needn't have bothered with the curtsy, as her second cousin was already halfway back to the library.

Hellfire.

Chapter Twenty-Three

Xander itched to dispense with the niceties before he could discuss the issues that had prompted his invitation. The marriage contract sat front and center on his desk although the men were across the room in the seating area, the duke on the settee that held fond memories of Evie laid out.

Hollibrook had excused himself for a minute, returning as the tea tray was brought in. Xander had learned that it was acceptable to have a servant pour, so he didn't have to fumble the fine china.

As the maid did so, his leg bounced impatiently. Even when the men noticed, he could not stop it.

Finally, the door closed behind the maid, and the men sipped their tea and chatted about the weather. Xander had to clench his fists to keep from knocking the china from their hands if they mentioned rain one more time.

Hollibrook lowered his cup to its saucer and eyed Xander. "Right, then. It seems your question is urgent. How can we help?"

Xander surged out of his seat to nab the contract off his desk. Waving it, he started, "I found this. 'Tis a contract to wed a Lady Evelyn Allen, daughter of the Earl of Craven."

Hollibrook crossed one leg over the other. "Ah, yes. She is my second cousin. My father's brother's granddaughter."

"Hmph." That stumped Xander. How could he ask for what he wanted given that familial connection? But if he wanted to marry his little maid, he'd have to not only discuss declining this contract with the Allen chit's second cousin, but with her father as well. Might as well forge ahead. "Munroe has given me to understand that there are ways to refuse if I do not wish to move forward?"

Hollibrook frowned. "Perhaps. 'Tis frowned on, though, and could have serious repercussions for her. You'd need to step carefully."

"Of course, I empathize with Miss Allen—"

"Lady Evelyn," Hollibrook corrected mildly.

Xander nodded and continued. "Lady Evelyn. But I don't know her. And I most certainly don't wish to marry her. That is why I need your assistance. There must be a way through this without causing her undue pain or distress."

Hollibrook shook his head. "I am not so sure."

The duke frowned a question at Hollibrook and opened his mouth. Hollibrook gave a tiny shake of his head and his companion flattened his lips.

"May I ask why you don't wish to marry Lady Evelyn? She's the daughter of an earl and grandniece of a duke. Besides, she is quite comely. She'd do well as your wife, knowing the Ton and London as she does."

"I hate the idea of wedding a stranger."

The duke gestured to Hollibrook and sat back. It appeared the marquess was to handle this. He turned to Xander. "What if you invited her family for a visit? You could get to know her and see."

Xander fidgeted. "The truth is, I have someone else in mind."

"Oh." Hollibrook frowned. "Someone from your hometown? Or the village here?"

"Not exactly." He shifted his eyes between the men. Searching for bravery, he heard Evie's voice say, "You're a duke," and took a breath.

The marquess leaned forward, still holding his cup and saucer. "As Lady Evelyn's relative, I'd appreciate the courtesy of you informing me of this other interest. Are you in love with this person?"

Xander was calm now. He nodded and said, "Yes, although I haven't told her that yet. I needed to speak with you about this contract."

"Come on, man. Enough pussyfooting around. Who in the world could you have met out here that would be an appropriate match for a duke?" The duke on the settee, whose name Xander could not remember, blinked, brows raised.

Xander frowned. "Define appropriate. I thought a duke could do what he likes, society be damned? She's helped me with Parliamentary bills, with societal rules around hosting, dining, and dancing, and even expectations."

Hollibrook appeared to be chewing on his cheek. "Who. Is. It?" he asked taking a sip from his tea.

Xander stifled his displeasure at being questioned. He'd have to deal with this sooner or later, especially if the man was Lady Evelyn's family. "A maid here, from the village. She was stationed in a London household for some time and has all sorts of useful knowledge as a result."

At Xander's first words, he spewed his mouthful of tea back into the cup, choking. Setting the cup down on the table next to him, he barked a laugh. "Ha. This is rich.

You want to throw over a duke's grandniece for a *maid*? I don't suppose it's the one who was in the front hall—petite, auburn hair, about twenty?"

Xander frowned. Jealousy consumed him at the detailed description. The marquess had no business noticing such details about his Evie. "Probably."

Wiping his face of tea with his handkerchief, the marquess shot his still silent companion an unfathomable look and said, "I really think you owe it to Lady Evelyn's family to meet them and her before making a decision."

Xander heaved a sigh. Another delay. "Fine. I shall write to them this afternoon. In the meantime, would you like a stroll of the gardens? I have other questions for you whilst you're here but they can wait until the morrow, as 'tis such a nice day."

* * * *

Xander lay awake for hours that night, waiting and hoping Evie would sneak into his room. The need to warn her of Hollibrook's requirements to respond to the betrothal was top of mind, but he was uncertain how to do so. And he wanted one more night of sensual exploration before having that conversation.

But she never came, despite his guests' rooms being in the other wing. The other servants seemed to accept their meetings, suppers, and dancing with equanimity, but he did not want to push his luck or her reputation by being caught sneaking around the servants' sleeping quarters on the third floor.

He'd told the guests that the house kept country hours but that they could of course request breakfast from the kitchen at whatever time they chose to arise. Their manservants had arrived a few hours behind them with their bags for their short stay.

So Xander awoke late and his guests rose early, and by the time they'd breakfasted and adjourned to the library to discuss farming issues they shared, he hadn't spied Evie.

Unfortunately, they referred him to Lancaster regarding the transferring the title for the pub to Banks, as documents such as that were filed through solicitors. The rest of the morning was spent on tenant farming disputes. For the most part the tenants were self-sufficient. When disputes arose, he didn't mind stepping in to settle them; it was similar to breaking up bar fights from his pub days. However, there were a few that were complex enough that recommendations on resolution from men with more experience were appreciated. If only his stepfather were closer. North was a gruff but fair man and was always happy to lend an ear or an opinion.

After lunch, they'd answered all his queries and offered to entertain themselves with a ride while he continued working through correspondence, in case he had more questions.

He was deep in Parliamentary language when a knock on the open library door brought his head up. Evie stood there, wringing her hands, that infernal cap askew on her head. "Your Grace, might I have a word?"

She was back to using his formal address, and he'd never seen her nervous before. Something was on her mind. His mind shifted from concern over the conversation he needed to have with her, to worry about whatever was bothering her. He gestured to a chair then the teapot on the corner of his desk. "Evie. Come in, come in. Tea? I can order fresh."

Despite her discomfort, she rolled her eyes. "I shall

remind you I'm not a guest. Although…"

When her voice trailed off, he tilted his head. "What is it? I missed you last night. Is aught amiss?"

Gazing at her hands twisted in her lap, she shook her head, nodded, then glanced up at him. "About being a guest—"

Again, a knock on the open door came. They both looked over. Rogers stood there looking perplexed. "My lord, you have guests, all the way from London. They seem to believe their daughter is here. Perhaps that is why they arrived without notice or invitation." The last sentence was grumbled.

Xander managed not to snicker at his servant's attitude when Xander himself was the most frequent breaker of societal mores of any titled nob.

Evie was up and standing by the door, peering out.

He hadn't seen her move. Something was definitely amiss. She was twitchy with nerves.

"Did you get their name?"

"The Earl and Countess of—"

Evie closed her eyes and held her breath, mouthing, "No, no, no, no."

Xander almost didn't hear Rogers's completion of the visitors' titles. "Craven, and Louisa Mullens."

He'd heard that last name before. Evie had given Mullens as her surname. But then why was this woman here with an Earl and his wife? And Craven was the title on the marriage contract. It appeared he might fulfill Hollibrook's wishes around breaking the betrothal quicker than he'd dared hope.

"Evie—" he started, but she'd slipped out past Rogers, tucked her head down, and run for the kitchen. "Rogers, please let Mrs. Betters know we have new guests who may or may not be staying. And I'll see them here. Ah, I guess do that in the reverse order. Thank you."

Rogers smiled. "Certainly, my lord."

Whatever their attitude toward his guests, Xander appreciated the servants' patience with him.

Chapter Twenty-Four

Oh no, oh no, oh no. Father and Mama had arrived, along with Aunt Lou. She needed to get Aunt Lou alone to find out why.

She paced the kitchen, wringing her hands, a new habit she'd formed in the last day since her second cousin had given her an ultimatum. His presence could escalate matters about the marriage contract.

Closing her eyes, she inhaled a huge breath and let it out slowly. She wanted Xander. He seemed to like her as a person, title aside. If they could get past her minor deception, they could marry quite soon. If he refused, she was not sure what she would do. One thing was certain. She would not allow her family to hold him to the contract against his wishes.

They were far enough from London that any compromising circumstances never need come to light, and she was still chaste, much to her chagrin and not for lack of trying.

An upstairs maid stepped into the kitchen. "Where are the guests?"

The girl looked askance at being questioned by a peer but answered in a mild tone. "His Grace offered them rooms, they accepted, and they are upstairs settling in before reconvening for tea when the marquess and duke return."

"Please, which rooms?" Evie asked.

"The front ones, so they are around the corner of the hall from the male guests."

"Aun—Mrs. Mullen, also?"

"Yes. Apparently she is family to the Countess of Craven, so although she is local she wanted to stay."

"Good." Evie started out of the kitchen but turned back. "Ah, ta."

She raced up the back stairs to Aunt Lou's room. Even before placing knuckles to wood, her aunt wrenched the door open and yanked her inside.

Evie threw herself into her aunt's arms. "Aunt Lou, 'tis so good to see you."

"And you as well. Hard work has not gotten the better of you, I see. How has your time here been? Your note was fractured…" her aunt's voice trailed off and pink rose in her cheeks.

"And interrupted. Don't think we won't speak of that," Evie said through laughter. "Later, though. I thought I asked for more time?"

"No. You ended with 'I need,' rather abruptly, I'm afraid. Whilst I won't apologize for what I do in the privacy of my home in my free time, I will say that the timing was rather unfortunate. I had to guess at what you needed, and the safer guess was bringing your parents here as soon as possible."

"Oh." Evie sagged. "I hadn't quite told him yet. And the Marquess of Hollibrook is here and recognized me as well. Auntie, I want Xander desperately. But I worry he shall be angry."

Louisa nodded. "He likely will. We talked about all of this when we decided on the plan. Anger will happen in a marriage from time to time. 'Tis how he resolves it that is important."

"I suppose."

"I cannot wait to hear about your time here. But for now, tell me. Do you love him?"

Evie sighed, smiling. "I thought I needed to speak to you about it, as I've never been in love. Honestly, though, I am quite sure. I am absolutely in love with him. More than London, more than influence in Parliament, more than caring that he is rough around the edges and may never wear a cravat for more than an hour. More than marriage."

"I'm so happy for you, my dear. That makes the stakes even higher, though. I hope he does not turn you out for lying," her aunt replied, tugging Evie toward the seating area by the fire.

"Well, yes, there is that." Evie stopped her aunt, who turned around to face her. Squeezing her hand, Evie begged, "Please, help me. What do I do?"

Louisa sighed. "I think we need your mother for this."

"She'll be furious." Evie grimaced.

"Yes. But she'll be on your side. She wants what is best for you. So she may berate you in private, but she'll champion you in public," Louisa said, patting her hand.

"First, though, I must find a way to tell Xander myself. I don't want him to hear it from an irate father or cousin or something."

"You'd best find him quickly then. Your mother will turn this house upside down looking for you if you don't show yourself soon—as Lady Evelyn."

"You have a few of my things with you?" At Lou's nod, Evie sighed. "Right. I'll go find my duke. Wish me luck."

* * * *

His lordship was in the library as always. Perhaps they should have some of their conversations around House of Lords decisions elsewhere. Otherwise, he might always associate this room with work. And it was a lovely room. Evie eyed the settee where he'd first introduced her to pleasure. A lovely room.

Focus, Evie. Stop procrastinating.

Xander looked up and saw her hovering in the doorway. At his welcoming smile, she sighed. Heavens, he was handsome. Still searching for words, she inched closer.

Forestalling anything she might say, he asked, "Is one of my latest guests a relation of yours, perhaps? You share a surname."

"Yes, actually." Evie answered honestly, although she knew he likely referred to Louisa Mullen, whose name she'd borrowed, rather than her mother.

"Oh? She's the sister of the Countess of Craven. Do they have another sister, and does she live near here? Should I invite her to visit?"

Her heart melted. He wanted her family to have a chance to visit with each other and her—a servant as far as he knew. Her Xander was truly a good man. Hands twisting and heart breaking, she slid her chin side to side, forming a negative response. "No other sister."

He frowned. "Then how can she be your aunt?"

"Xander." His brows shot up at her use of his given name, something she'd only done a handful of times and only in bed when she forgot herself. "Please. I did all this with the best of intentions. For both of us—well, mostly for me, but anyway. I lied to you about my last name."

He was frowning now. "Why?"

Evie opened her mouth to respond, but her mother's

voice echoed in the hall. "Evie? You, there. My sister told me that Evie was staying here, but no one knows of a guest named Evelyn."

Rogers murmured something Evie couldn't hear. Her breaking heart threatened to beat out of her chest, yet she was frozen, unable to form the words she needed to warn Xander.

"Well, then, where is the duke, please? I need to understand what is going on here."

Evie heaved a sigh, resigned. She'd done this to herself, waiting too long before confessing. She stood and faced the doorway, waiting for the inevitable.

Rogers appeared, likely to tell the duke that the countess wished for an audience, but Evie's mother pushed past him. "Evie! There you—whatever are you wearing?"

Flashing a side glance at Xander, Evie stepped forward to hug her mother. "Mama. I've missed you. And I have a lot to tell you and the duke. Might we get tea please, Rogers?"

He nodded as though she'd been a visiting lady all along and reversed his direction to inform the kitchen.

Xander stood behind his desk, eyes flicking between her and her mother.

"My lord, would you join us by the fireplace?" She gestured to the seating area.

He raised his brows already having learned that even an earl's daughter shouldn't be directing a duke, much less in his own home.

But he acquiesced, coming around the desk and choosing a chair. His expression was unreadable, as though he had erected a wall between them. Her heart ached at the idea.

The ladies perched on the settee. Evie's backbone snapped extra-straight, not touching the back of the sofa, just as a lady would in any drawing room she visited. It was as though she'd always been here as herself in an alternate reality. Or else this was a dream.

A footman brought in the tea tray. As if it was the most natural thing in the world, Evie said, "Thank you. I'll pour."

Her mother snatched the annoying cap off Evie's head and breathed a sigh of relief. "Lud, your hair is too tight, you'll give yourself a headache. But I was afraid you'd cut it all off or something. Now, *please*, someone tell me what is going on here."

"Yes, I'd like to know as well." Xander spoke for the first time since her mother's appearance, his voice a rumble through tight lips.

Evie handed them their cups and saucers and left hers down. Fisting her hands in her servant's garb, she took a deep breath and started. "My lord, as you may have guessed by now, my name is Evelyn Allen. This is my mother, and Louisa, who lives in the village, is my aunt."

Her mother narrowed her eyes and muttered, "I'd wager LouLou had something to do with this, too."

Evie hastened to add, "Mother, this was my idea. Please don't blame Aunt Louisa or the duke. He hired me as a servant and has treated me—and all his staff—very well."

"You're here without a chaperone! That is not treating you with the respect you deserve."

"He didn't know."

Xander opened his mouth to say something, but she sent him a pleading glance. Glaring at her, he subsided.

"He had no idea. I did this because I was young and

stupid when I asked for the betrothal to the previous duke but regretted it when I discovered his Tory leanings. And yes, I know Papa has a few, but he listens to you and is fair, at least most of the time. That is what I want in a marriage, and Xand—his lordship was a complete unknown. I needed to see where his politics lay."

"So you came here as a *maid*?" Her mother screeched the question at a near-shout.

Evie saw Xander grimace at her mother's tone, but she'd expected it. Ignoring the escalating volume, she answered in what she hoped were calming tones. "Yes. It's honest work. I've learned a lot that I'll share with you for your household."

"And?" Her mother cast a look at Xander, her voice closer to normal again.

Xander was done waiting at that point. He bit out, "So you're telling me you lied to me about your identity and were spying on me in my own house?"

"Yes." Evie bowed her head for a moment. "I apologize, my lord. Women have very little say in their decisions which affect their world, and I hoped to at least influence who I was to spend the rest of my life with. You must understand a little, no? You've voiced how appalled you are at some of the bills that Parliament passes that burden the working class, without giving them a choice."

He glared again. "They are open about it. They don't sneak around and spy on people in their own homes. And anyway, they're nobs. I expect it of them. Which I suppose fits this situation as well." The last sentence was said through a sneer. He turned to her mother. "'Tis good you are here, Madam. I don't know if you received my invitation, but I wanted to tell you that I am unable to honor the marriage contract with your daughter. I shall work out the particulars with your husband later. Now, if you'll excuse me—"

Without finishing his excuse or waiting for an answer, he stood and walked out of the room.

Evie wanted to run after him, to beg and cry, but she knew Xander often needed time to process conundrums. And she'd created an enormous tangle. Guilt wilted her stiff posture, and she sniffed, reaching for a handkerchief she didn't carry in her maid's uniform. Grabbing her mobcap, she swiped at her tears with it and avoided her mother's angry gaze.

She had counted on Xander being angry but forgiving her, certain he felt as she did. She'd seen a future of her helping him with correspondence, him teaching her even more in the bedroom. He hadn't even taken an hour to consider her reasons for the deception, refusing the marriage outright.

Now what?

Chapter Twenty-Five

Xander was going to break a cask open if he kept throwing them around like this. But there was nothing else around to burn out his ire. He'd always deep cleaned or found casks to rearrange at the pub when he was angry or thinking through something.

His lips twisted as the morning's conversation replayed in his head. He'd need to speak to the earl, but at least his intentions were clear. With luck, they were packing to leave on the morrow. If not, he'd make himself scarce again.

Movement in the corner of his eye brought his head around. The Marquess of Hollibrook stood by the pub's back door, arms folded.

Xander lifted his chin and stomped over. "How did you find me?"

"Your valet. You do realize 'tis not good form to abandon guests at your house?"

"They were not invited," Xander grumped.

"And myself and my colleague?" The Marquess raised his brows, but his tone remained mild.

"Right. My apologies. Are you aware of this morning's…" he was at a loss for how to describe it.

"Revelations? Actually, I was aware of the issue yesterday. I recognized Evie in the front hall."

Xander groaned, turning away and running a hand through his hair. He'd not get sympathy from this quarter then. He muttered, "So much for the Wayward Dukes Alliance, eh?"

Hollibrook snorted. "My cousin's wife and her sister are a bit mad, if you ask me, and they've raised Evie to that standard. I understand your dilemma."

"So you'll help?"

"If you really need me to. But Rutland, the Alliance is here to save you from scheming young ladies, families, and the like. I know I appear biased, but I can tell you these particular females may be mad, but their intentions are pure."

"Pure intentions would not include lies to one's intended husband."

"Come now. When we first met, you were going to meet the 'chit' and evaluate whether you wanted her. This visit, you were ready to throw her over without a thought for a maid. Even in a backwater pub in the wilds of Northumberland, you must have seen how little freedom women have in this world. When it comes to choosing one's husband, most titled young ladies have less say than working-class girls. She wanted the same thing you wanted—a chance to evaluate your fit as a husband. And look how good a fit it turned out to be."

Xander tried, but all he could conjure was every time Evie laughed at his ineptness as a duke. Offering a servant tea, not offering visitors a drink, and on and on. He'd taken her humor as joining him in seeing the ridiculousness of dukes' entitlement. Now he could see it had been mirth at his expense. "I cannot abide lies. I hated the damned aristocracy until I became one of them—you. And the two together are beyond redemption."

"Like it or not, even for a duke, wedding a maid

would have caused a scandal. This solves your dilemma perfectly. You marry the girl you *love*—your word, if you recall—and still fulfill the marriage contract."

"I could never love someone who lied to me."

* * * *

Hollibrook had had no response to his declaration. So after the evening meal, Xander called the earl and the marquess into his office. Hollibrook had agreed to mediate. He'd also asked Xander to include Evie in the meeting, but Xander refused. He could barely look at her over the supper table without losing his appetite to fury.

He directed his guests to the seating area by the fireplace, although he'd given serious thought to having this tense exchange from behind the safety of his desk. Pouring three whiskies, he ignored the memory of learning that from Evie, passed two to the others, and sat.

"Your Grace," the earl started without waiting for niceties or protocol. "I am given to understand from my wife that you are declining my request to honor the marriage contract. Is that correct?"

"Yes," Xander answered. He'd studied the Earl of Craven over supper. Evie was a mirror image of her mother, except for the set of her mouth. It wasn't the shape as much as the expressions. In another setting, he'd want to joke with her father to see if her enchanting laugh came from him.

"Yet my daughter has been living in your house for a month without a chaperone." That expressive mouth flattened.

"Yes. By her choice and without my consent or awareness." Xander laid out the facts in a flat tone, fighting to keep his calm. Defensiveness would not help his case.

"You'll find that doesn't matter to many in the Ton, unfortunately." The earl shook his head once, the blond strands moving in a motion similar to Evie's darker tresses. "She'll still be considered well and truly compromised. I realize the circumstances are less than ideal, but please think of her reputation."

Xander replied, "The marquess has informed me that he thinks we are far enough north that scandal can be avoided if we end this quietly and I do not come to London for a few months."

The earl shot a look at his cousin. "Holly. You're taking his side?"

"He has a lot on his plate at the moment, Elliot. I've asked him to consider not taking action until after the Season."

Craven nodded. "That would give them time to see she's not with child, should it come to that."

"What?" Xander roared, shooting to stand. "Surely, you've spoken with your daughter about this. She'll tell you she cannot be pregnant—at least not by me."

Craven stood, too, balling his fists at his sides. "Duke or no, I'll thank you to keep a civil tongue in your head when it comes to my daughter. I never said she might be pregnant. But London is all about appearances, and they need proof. Even so, if word gets out about this, she's done for."

Xander shook his head. "You cannot have it both ways. Either we are remote and quiet enough that we avoid rumors, or it won't matter whether she's expecting."

Hollibrook jumped in. "Look, I understand your frustration—" At Xander's doubtful look, he added,

"Family or not, I do comprehend it. But the more time we can put between you becoming duke and her stay here versus a broken betrothal, the better it is. People forget, including the people closer to Rutland, and new scandals arise. If Evie returns to London with her family now, then the contract is broken after the Season, it will help everyone."

"How will it help me?"

"For one, it will allow you time to establish your presence in the House of Lords, even if you do it from here. If you are able to accumulate like-minded allies there, they can smooth your path into society when you come to Town. Evie has her circle of friends, as do her parents. They can support the message of voiding the old contract upon the prior duke's death as a mutual agreement between the families."

Xander suspected it would reinforce the view that he was an upstart, a working-class man who didn't belong with the London set, but he couldn't care less. He was still scrambling to learn everything required to do the most good for the men and women of England who needed his support—people like him from humble origins who could benefit from his representation. Not the liars of the London set.

However, despite her duplicity, he didn't want Evie's reputation to be irrevocably smeared. He nodded his acquiescence, taking a gulp of whiskey.

Chapter Twenty-Six

Desperate, Evie waited until the household was quiet to trace her nightly path to Xander's bedroom.

Anxiety that he wouldn't hear her out threatened to choke her. Holding her breath, she depressed the lever of the door handle. Locked. Her fears had been well-founded.

She shrugged. The guests, including her family, were around a corner of the hall. The staff had accepted both her and Xander's unique perspectives on their supposed "stations." So she knocked softly and spoke close to the door. "Xander, please let me apologize."

Silence.

"Xander," she tried a little louder. "Please."

She debated going to see if she could find Mrs. Betters's keyring, but she didn't want to anger Xander any further.

She knocked again.

A rustle of fabric through the door signified movement, but the lock did not click open.

Almost nose-to-wood, she said, "I want to explain."

At that, the door was yanked open. "You explained already. Forgive me for not finding your excuses acceptable." He shrugged and added, "Or don't."

She lifted a foot to step forward, not wanting to have this conversation in the hall, but Xander stepped into her space, blocking the doorway.

"Oh no." He narrowed his eyes and spoke through gritted teeth. "You don't get to come in here and say I compromised you. You wished to speak to me, do it here, or like your so-called civilized peers like to say, visit at a decent hour with a chaperone present."

She sighed. Seeing the situation from his viewpoint, his lack of trust made sense, but it still hurt. She'd anticipated that he'd be calmer by now, but she'd caused him a mix of embarrassment and pain. Squaring her shoulders, she hoped he'd listen to her explanation and find some resonance with his own situation. "Please imagine a young, impressionable girl—"

He snorted and folded his arms across his chest.

"—of ten-and-seven in her first season. She has a decent dowry and thus is the belle of all the balls. Then a surprisingly young duke—a duke!—pays her attention. And he doesn't need her dowry, so he must like her for herself."

"Sounds like the normal shallow-minded self-centeredness of the Ton."

Evie stamped her foot, and his brows rose. He unfolded his arms as though to close the door between them.

Taking a deep breath, she forced herself to remain calm but spoke faster in fear he'd stop listening and shut her out. "I believe I mentioned she was young and impressionable. And very sheltered. 'Twas only after the papers were signed that she understood his nature. He was a bigot and a snob, and he expected her to be silent, acquiescing to his direction at all times. And, once there were children, likely out of sight in a country home like this one whilst he sowed his wild oats in London."

Re-crossing his arms, he drew his mouth to the side,

looking skeptical.

She threw out her hands and begged, "How could I have known? Navigating the politics of London for a young débutante was like—like you navigating the House of Lords decisions needing your input. If you hadn't had help would you have known what questions to ask?"

He narrowed his eyes.

She hoped that meant he was thinking. "I came with the best of intentions—"

He snorted again, indicating she'd lost what little sympathy he might have felt.

"I did," she insisted. "Please, if nothing else, believe that. I didn't want to be miserable. Nor did I want you to be wed to someone who didn't suit you. Let's be honest, I'm not the quiet demure type. I was never going to sit quietly by whilst my husband made atrocious decisions that hurt our country and caroused with other women."

His lips twitched as the corners of his lips betrayed him. He was clearly suppressing a smile.

"Before your predecessor died, I was already looking for a way out of the marriage. I was frantic. Then you inherited and no one knew a thing about you. Xander, you know me." She was wringing her hands now in frustration and earnestness. "I am the last person to care about your background. I simply wanted to know if you were a good man."

The still-silent duke continued staring at her. It was time to be brave. She stepped in, toe to toe with him, laying a hand on his forearms, just in front of his heart. "And Xander, you *are* a good man. The best of men. And somewhere along the way, I fell in love with you."

"Ha!"

The bark of laughter made her blink and step back. His response to her confessing her love was laughter. A knife twisted in her chest. He wasn't going to forgive her.

He continued at full voice, "Fine. You asked me to believe you had the best of intentions—if nothing else. That is all I'm willing to believe of all this nonsense. You are here because you decided you want the pub manager duke for some reason. Perhaps I am a trophy. Perhaps 'tis to save face. Perhaps—" he leaned in and lowered his voice a degree. "—'twas the bedroom lessons. Whatever, I'm not falling for the ruse. Dealing with being a nob after hating them all is bad enough. I don't need to abide liars."

With that, he stepped back and slammed the door, leaving Evie inches from it alone in the hall. She stared at it, motionless, wishing she could have told him earlier, or finished that note to Aunt Lou, or had one more chance to hold him. The clank of glass behind the door meant he'd moved on from their conversation, pouring himself a drink in all likelihood. She returned to her servant quarters with tears streaming down her face and her heart shattered.

* * * *

Evie sat with her mother and aunt in the sitting room off her parents' bedroom, perched on the footstool between their chairs. A tea tray and cups sat abandoned on the table behind her.

She'd chosen this seat against her mother's admonishments about ladylike behavior so she could be within touching distance of her favorite relatives. Lud, she'd missed these ladies. Despite her joy at seeing them again, her eyes stung and were swollen despite the cold compresses of tea she'd kept on them for a half hour this morning.

Her mother sat with lips pressed together and her hands gripping her knees. "Evie, whatever were you thinking?"

"I was about to tell him. I'd hoped for a few more days, but cousin Hollie arrived and caught me."

"I'm talking about all these weeks, not the past day. You have everything a girl could want—pretty dresses, an account at the bookstore, friends. Yet you are up here scrubbing floors and whatever else."

"You saw what happened. The previous duke was all smiles and courtly manners until he had Father's signature on the marriage contract. Then he became dictatorial and standoffish if I stepped so much as a toe out of line. Plus, he was a *Tory*. I told you and Father I wanted to break the contract, and you said to bide my time. As though I was being flighty."

"You'll excuse us if we worried you'd change your mind yet again. You'd already changed it once in a matter of a month."

"Based on *his* behavior." Aunt Lou stepped in to defend her, and Evie squeezed her knee in thanks.

Mama waved a hand. "I suppose that is all beside the point now, anyway. How could you believe this was the solution though?"

"How else? Xander is still prevaricating about coming to London. He hates the place and the aristocracy, and he is struggling with all of this change."

"Can't say I blame him," Aunt Lou murmured.

Mama shot her sister a quelling look before asking Evie, "And what did you discover?"

"Oh, Mama," Evie breathed out. "He is the kindest

person I know. Gruff, certainly, and rough. But ever so kind under that tough exterior. He ensures the staff have time off, more than any other household I've seen. He keeps his meals simple. The whole household is in awe of him yet comfortable enough that they'll help him if he stumbles on a certain aspect of ducal etiquette."

Louisa sighed through a smile, propping her chin in her hand.

Mama glanced at her and allowed herself a small smile also. "I'm starting to see."

Excited that her family was so enraptured with the idea of romance, Evie was still waxing poetic. "He always checks that I am comfortable."

"When would he need to worry about that?" Her mother's voice went sharp.

Evie jolted and slanted a guilty glance at her mother. "When we are reading by candlelight in the evenings, of course. I thought I mentioned that I've helped him with Parliamentary correspondence?"

"No, you had not. What is this, then? And how did it come about?"

Evie heaved a sigh of relief at having redirected her mother's attention and explained, as Mama and Aunt Lou exchanged knowing looks.

Her mother tilted her head and said more than asked, "You're in love with him."

Evie burst into noisy tears yet again, nodding as she was unable to form words.

Both ladies leaned forward to rub her back. Her mother said, "Sometimes a strategic retreat is the way to win the war. I think we should move to the inn in town, and you can stay with your aunt. The duke has agreed to wait until after the Season to dissolve the agreement, so we have time to formulate a new battle plan."

* * * *

The following morning, the ladies sat in a private room at the inn, where Evie shared a sofa with her mother and her aunt lounged across from them. Evie was in a gown she'd brought from London, chafing at the layers of undergarments and restrictions, despite the fineness of the fabrics.

The clothing inspired her mood. She'd cried all her tears at Xander's. For herself for her stupidity, for Xander's unwillingness to understand her predicament, and for her broken heart.

Lady Evelyn Allen was ready to plan.

Her mother poured tea for the three of them while fixing Evie with a stern look. "If you were so sure you wanted him as a husband, why did you not admit your ruse? Look at your hands, so rough from all that hard work. It will already take ages to make you presentable again. Why stay and continue to work as a"—she could barely form the words—"as a—servant?"

Evie sighed. The right answer was probably not *because I was having fun and learning all sorts of intimate activities besides.* Choosing more diplomatic words, she answered, "There was always more to learn."

"And now?"

"Now," Evie said with an even heavier sigh, "I cannot imagine ever learning enough to want to leave. Xander is compelling. He champions the working class whilst being willing to learn to navigate the clubs and ballrooms of London rather than burning the world down. I considered myself enlightened until I heard his take on some of these laws. He challenges me, he teaches me, and he is open to learning from me."

When she finished trying to describe her feelings, Aunt Lou began to clap, and her mama had tears in her eyes.

Mama dabbed at her eyes. "Right, then. How do we change his mind on honoring the marriage?"

Evie wrapped an arm around her mother to hug her. Her mother's acceptance of this whole crazy scheme and offer to help plan their next steps gave her hope. "Thank you, Mama."

"Perhaps you insist—I mean, invite—His Grace to London and introduce him to society?" Louisa tossed out.

Mama shook her head. "That could damage Evie's reputation more if he continues on this path of refusing the marriage."

Evie added her thoughts. "Xander hates London. It might be more than we can hope for to overcome that, especially given his hatred of both 'nobs' and the city."

"Letters, perhaps? Keeping the conversation open?" Mama asked.

"No." Aunt Lou straightened her spine. "In person is always better. She needs to stay here."

"Oh, dear. I don't know that Elliot will allow that."

"I have faith in you, sister. You'll find a way to convince him."

"After all this mess? I'm not so sure." Her mother went to find the earl, only to return and inform them that he was already ordering the servants to pack their things and was adamant they return to London—with Evie.

Chapter Twenty-Seven

Betrayal by a trusted friend was the worst sort. Perfidy by someone he'd thought he'd loved was beyond imaginable. He'd confided in Evie, allowed her to see his failings and lack of confidence, and bared his soul to her as much as his body. Blazes, he'd relied on her to direct his votes in Parliament. Now Xander was questioning everything.

Of course, once he'd learned she was Ton, it all made sense. Duplicitous through and through, the lot of them.

To think he'd considered breaking off his betrothal—with her—in order to marry her. He frowned. 'Twas the extremity of his luck that such a sentence could make sense. No one else would believe it.

Finally free of houseguests, including the little servant-turned-liar, Xander wasted no time informing his staff that he'd be traveling to Northumberland. In all the chaos of discovering Evie's identity, he'd not had a moment to write to Jacob Lancaster, so he'd do that from his stepfather's.

In a private conversation, he checked with Fletcher on what members of the household typically traveled with a duke, and in a separate talk with Munroe, he assured the steward of his faith in his management skills. After all, Munroe oversaw it quite well before Xander had arrived.

With everything as settled as he could manage, they

departed. The weather was thankfully too uncertain for him to be expected to ride a horse, so he could sit in the carriage without losing face. It was only a two-day ride to his family.

At the castle, the footman who answered the door informed him that his mother was pacing the floor; she'd been hovering in the great hall for two hours.

Indeed, he spied her over the servant's shoulder. Her familiar loving face comforted him. Here, he didn't have to be in charge. It helped that he knew from her letters that North treated her like a queen and their marriage was happy.

She rushed him as soon as he removed his overcoat. "Xander, I was so pleased to get your note. We'd hesitated to come to you until we'd heard from you that you'd settled into your new home. And look at you."

He'd worn a cravat and waistcoat that day, despite the long hours in a coach that made him want to rip it off and open his collar, as he'd known it would make her happy. Her step back and head tilt to admire him made him smirk and spread his arms. "Look at me, Mama. A godforsaken duke."

She gasped. "Oh my boy. Are you still angry about joining the Terrible Ton as you called them?"

"A little." He shrugged. "There's been a complication I wanted to discuss with you and North if he's available."

"He's here, just out meeting with some tenants at the moment. Perhaps tomorrow? Can we have today to enjoy being together? Your brother is due for supper as well."

"That sounds lovely. Thank you, Mama," he said with a kiss to her cheek.

In the end, a question from his brother about heirs

brought out the marriage contract dilemma and the subterfuge of his potential bride, so the discussion did not wait for the morning.

Eleanor quizzed him about Evie, Bruce asked if he'd been attracted to her, and North leaned back in his chair and listened, sipping wine.

Eleanor clapped her hands. "I like her. I want to meet her."

Xander shook his head, catching North doing the same but with a smile. "Haven't you been listening, Mama? She deceived me for weeks. I don't plan on ever seeing her again."

"I wouldn't go that far," North said, his first words on the subject. "London is a small town in many ways. When you're in Town for Parliament or estate business, there is an expectation that you attend at least a few social gatherings. As a duke, you'll have even more pressure than me."

Eleanor jumped in. "She helped you. I still want to meet her, although I hate London nearly as much as you do."

As the earl's second wife, and a commoner, she was unaccustomed to the hours, the expectations, and the snobbery she'd encountered on her first two trips south. She had been quite vocal about her desire to avoid the place as often as her husband's station allowed.

"You may get your wish, my dear," North rumbled. Turning to Xander, he added, "It appears you're ready for me to introduce you to some allies in Lords and help you sift through some of the invitations likely waiting for you at your London home."

* * * *

They sent a note ahead to Xander's London household to allow them to prepare for his arrival, while he caught his family up on what he'd learned and life as a duke. Bruce snorted with laughter at his description of his escapes to the pub. The few days were the most relaxed he'd been in months. But while Northumberland and family were familiar and comfortable, he took time to scribble a note to Munroe about his next destination, and a separate note to Mrs. Betters to ensure she had everything she needed. He already thought of Rutland and its people as home.

Upon arriving in London, they walked through Xander's house in the heart of Mayfair. He marveled again at the excessive opulence. Dukes had to entertain, and some of his predecessors had had families. But it still felt like too much wasted space that could house more people, and an accumulation of wood that would need polishing by a maid with a heart-shaped bottom. No, he needed to stop thinking of her, particularly as a maid.

North's London home was on the eastern edge of that neighborhood. Luke and his wife Belle stayed in the home she'd already owned when they met, several neighborhoods away, close to where he'd bought property for the group home. Luke and Belle came for visiting hours on their first full day in Town, and Xander was struck by the fact that both North's and Luke's wives were untitled before they married. In fact, Belle, ten years older than Luke, had been a courtesan, and North had been one of her clients.

It was proof that his idea of marrying a maid hadn't been as outlandish as he'd feared. And of course, Evie was not actually a maid. The ascension to titles was also proof that he'd be accepted by some despite his background, if not all. Perhaps one day the city would not make him itch for a country village.

North had wanted to wait to go through the invitations for Luke and Belle's arrival. Xander was surprised when Belle was the one to sort the pile, although on second thought, he realized he shouldn't be. She knew more about the Ton than any of them, having spent more time in London and much of that socializing, albeit not always in polite circles.

She barely glanced at the senders' names before putting them into three piles. "Bigot, snob, coxcomb, outright cove," were apparently the "no" pile. Slags, clodhoppers, and eccentrics were maybes. There were only three yeses. Luke's best friend William, the Earl of Harrington, was having a birthday party; she seemed to think Xander had been invited due to his familial connection to Luke. Belle noted that the Earl of Cheltenham, who she referred to as Cheltie, would be there, and called him the most important man in London to know, with William's wife a close second. They were friends and between the two of them, they had funded a good chunk of the small businesses in London, especially those owned by women. In fact, Cheltie had met his wife that way.

The other two invitations were for fêtes held by members of the House of Lords' Whig party who could be important allies, one of which was before the birthday celebration. North knew them both, although Luke did not. He was happy to leave the running of the earldom and politics to his father as much as North allowed, so he could focus on his own enterprise.

Belle slanted him a look, glancing at Xander's rather loosely tied cravat. "Do you have appropriate London attire?"

"Probably not."

She nodded. "We shall get you sorted. In the meantime, tell me what brought you down?"

So Xander had to relay the story once again.

Belle nodded throughout. "I don't know that I'll be able to find out if the Craven clan will be at any of these." She tapped the three prioritized invitations. "Are you prepared to encounter them? Do they know you're in Town?"

Xander nodded, then shook his head.

"Given that no clarification of the marriage contract has been made publicly, courtesy demands that you send a note informing them. You'd normally be expected to visit as well, but I think we can forego that."

He sighed, belatedly recalling what a force of nature she was. Luke's charitable project had been expedited due to her connections and no-nonsense attitude. "What else?"

"North, I assume you'll introduce him at your club and ensure the transition of membership?"

"If needed. We're meeting with his London solicitor tomorrow on a number of matters, and he may have already arranged for that at wherever the previous duke was a member."

"I'll get an appointment with a tailor by tomorrow morning. After that, you'll be so busy you won't have a moment to breathe. Take it one interaction, one person at a time, and I can come by each morning to go over who you've met and what their story is, even if Luke is at the other house."

"Thank you." He took a deep breath and looked around the room. If he had to deal with London and nobs, he had the best supporters around him he could ask for. Barring Evie, anyway. Reminding himself she was a liar, he repeated, "Thank you all for your love and support."

Chapter Twenty-Eight

After her father's mandate, the family had been packed and whisked off to London posthaste. Evie spent the entire trip and the fortnight since missing Xander and worrying that she'd never convince him she'd meant well.

Her mother attempted once again to convince her to join her on an outing to the modiste, claiming Evie desperately needed new gowns. Evie pictured the wardrobe in her room and her dressing room and could not imagine why her mother thought such a thing. Regardless, she was not interested. She'd worn two dresses up north, swapping them out to clean and air them, and hadn't expired from lack of variety.

Mama had brought her jar upon jar of creams for her hands. Evie used them when she remembered. She did enjoy having her skin be soft and supple again, rather than chapped and feeling as though it was stretched too tight over her hands. But she was out of the habit of these time-consuming, inane rituals and couldn't find the interest to re-engage in them.

In so many ways, London and its expectations seemed far shallower and senseless with her recent experiences and seeing it through Xander's eyes.

Indeed, she hadn't mustered up interest in any of her old practices, except one. She read the newspapers manically, and even sat in her father's office reading

Parliamentary bills when he didn't have need of them.

The rest of her days, she moped. There was no other word for it. She knew her parents worried. And she should likely join them for a few of the parties they attended, to show London society she was happy and carefree. Assuming Xander would eventually decline the contract, she needed to remain fresh in the London set's minds in order to find another husband.

None of it could be imagined, though. Not being happy or carefree and certainly not marrying anyone other than Xander. Her heart was broken, and she had no idea how long it would take to mend, if ever.

Two events loomed that her parents insisted she attend, as they were organized by close political allies. If she had to socialize, forward-thinking MPs were her first choice. Perhaps she could mention that Xander's views lay in their direction, based on a "recent visit to his country home with her family."

She shook her head, frustrated. After such a thorough rejection, why contemplate ways in which to help him?

She rationalized with herself. *'Tis for the greater good of the country.*

So she sat through the primping, patting, and pinning for the first party. In the carriage ride, her mother ran through the names and titles of the people most likely to attend. Then came the air kisses, and gloved hand squeezes, and empty platitudes.

Evie snuck a glass of champagne when her parents were pulled away and sighed.

Another of her father's friends who was standing nearby smiled and said, "That is a rather heavy sigh for such a young lady."

"La, sir. We all have our troubles. My hair didn't curl

correctly tonight."

"Now, Lady Evelyn, I know you better than that. You are your father's daughter. I'm guessing it was something weightier than that."

"Well, yes. Have you corresponded with the new Duke of Rutland, sir?"

"Rutland, Rutland," he said with a pensive look. "I believe so."

"I think you'll find his politics similar to your own; you might find him an ally. And when he visits London, he'll be looking for an entrée into the clubs and soirées."

"How do you know this, child?"

"My family visited him briefly last month. I…overheard the men discussing Lords' business one afternoon."

He chuckled. "Truly your father's daughter."

The servant at the ballroom doors announced the next guest. "The Duke—"

The crowd hushed. Evie managed not to roll her eyes. Ah, London. No wonder Xander had no patience for it. The man could be the cruelest, most horrible person in the world but they'd pander to him based on that four-letter word.

"—of Rutland."

Evie's jaw dropped even before Xander stepped through the door, clenching and unclenching his hands by his sides. He wanted to fidget, to rip the cravat from around his neck, she could see it all flit through his eyes.

Instead, he stepped into the room without meeting anyone's eyes, as his stepfather and mother were announced. Murmurs rose on a swell as heads leaned toward each other, reminding their companions who North was to Xander and how it all came to be.

The older statesman turned to her. "That was quite the party trick, Lady Evelyn. 'Tis as though you conjured him." He bowed his head. "If you'll excuse me, I shall find your father and ask for an introduction."

Within a quarter hour, Xander and North were surrounded by Members of Parliament, talking and gesturing. Evie pictured standing by his side listening, or more likely rousing, the wives on whatever subject was at hand. Dragging her gaze from him, she saw North's wife sitting against the wall chatting with another lady.

Evie's mother, standing with a beautiful lady somewhere between her and her mother's age, gestured Evie over.

"Countess, may I present my daughter, Lady Evelyn. Evie, this is Lady Charlotte, Countess of Harrington."

Evie curtsied. "My lady, 'tis a pleasure."

"Lovely to meet you. Please call me Charlotte, and may I call you Evie? I hate standing on formality."

Evie blinked. She liked this woman already. She'd heard about her in London circles, as the former Countess of Peterborough who managed the estate's finances and was one of the wealthiest people—man or woman—in England as a result. She had married the Earl of Harrington and brought the Harrington estate back from ruin by the previous earl, in between bearing an heir and a spare.

"Your mother tells me you are betrothed to the Duke of Rutland."

Evie shot her mother a sharp look. "I was betrothed to the previous duke. The new duke is…well, new."

Charlotte smiled. "Well put."

The small orchestra began warming up.

Charlotte said, "That is my cue to find my husband.

Ladies, might I presume to call on you tomorrow?"

Her mother accepted with alacrity.

The musical instruments made Evie gulp in fear. She was not yet ready to face Xander. Worse, she might cast up her accounts if he danced with another woman. There was no doubt he'd be very much in demand with the débutantes and their mothers. "Mama, please. I have a sore head, and the music is making it worse. Might we leave now?

Her mother eyed her suspiciously, no doubt wishing to ask if her head had begun to hurt when Xander arrived, but went to find the earl and make their excuses. He stayed, opting to go to his club with a few cronies later.

She escaped to the carriage, sinking into the corner of the squabs and closing her eyes, unable to fathom a time when she would be free of the pain of loss.

* * * *

Evie picked at the skirt of her gown, wiggling in her chair until her mother admonished her. "Do read or knit or something, Evie."

She could not concentrate, nervous about the Countess of Harrington's visit. Perhaps she should have claimed that her headache continued.

It was too late, however. She was here and dressed, and someone was knocking at the front door.

There were no less than three calling cards, reading, "The Countess of Harrington," "Lady Lynwood," and the scariest, "The Countess of Northumberland."

Mama gasped and nodded at the footman while Evie reeled. Her head might start to hurt for real at this rate. She did not recognize the name Lady Lynwood, but her bigger concern was why Xander's mother was with the nice Charlotte she'd met last night and what they wanted from her.

She stood stiffly, loitering behind her mother until the older woman turned and grabbed her arm to drag her forward and introduce her.

"Lady Charlotte, you remember Evie."

"'Tis simply Charlotte, please."

Her mother nodded and simpered. Evie wanted to step on her toes and run from the room.

Charlotte turned, gesturing to the oldest woman first whom Evie recalled entering with the Earl of Northumberland the night before. Charlotte could introduce her however she pleased, but to Evie, this was Xander's mother and thus the most important person in the room.

The buzzing of nerves through her made it difficult to hear the introduction, but she caught the older woman's words, "...call me Eleanor."

"And I am Patience, and this is Evie."

"Last but not least, my best friend in the world, Belle Lynwood. She is also wife to North's son, Luke. Luke and my husband, William, are the closest of friends, which is super convenient," Charlotte said with a light laugh.

"Oh yes, I can see how that would be lovely." Evie swore her mother was going to start drooling, she was so happy to have new friends for Evie. Her mama was worried about allaying any gossip and future marriage prospects should the contract with Xander fall apart. She didn't know how to tell her mother these women would be on Xander's side, no matter what happened.

Tea was brought and poured as the women exchanged pleasantries about the prior evening.

When the maid stepped out, Charlotte sat back and stared straight at Evie. "I suspect you know why we're here."

"I was surprised to see Xan—the Duke of Rutland in Town," Evie parried. If they were here to condemn her for her behavior, she'd be damned if she bowed and scraped. She stood by her actions.

"I can well imagine. We were just as surprised—pleasantly so—to see Eleanor and North. Right, Belle?" she asked with a sly grin.

Belle shot her a look, and Eleanor snorted and coughed into her teacup.

Interesting. There was some story there, but Evie was certain she wouldn't be privy to it anytime soon.

"Of course. It's always lovely to have one's husband's parents appear on your doorstep with one day's notice," Belle said, making a silly face at Eleanor.

"Now, now, dear. It could be worse. We could stay in your guest room instead of having our own home here," Eleanor replied smartly. She turned to Evie, "But we digress. My son has explained what transpired over the past two months, or at least his version of it. We've come to hear your side."

Evie ignored her mother's gape at Eleanor's boldness and squared her shoulders. These women were Xander's family and friends. It would do no good to speak badly of him, not to mention her lingering desire to regain his trust. "There aren't sides. I lied to him. I am sure what he told you was the truth; he's a very fair man."

Eleanor's brows rose, and a slow smile grew on her lips. "He is. But he's had some unpleasant experiences with "nobs" as he likes to refer to them, and I worry it's colored his view of events."

"That's right—" Evie turned to Belle—"your husband began a recovery program for those with…dependencies. How is that progressing?"

Belle raised a finger and wagged it. "Eh, eh, eh. We can discuss that next visit. First, let's see what the situation is and how we can help."

"Shouldn't you be talking to Xa—His Grace about that?"

"We have," Eleanor reinserted herself in the conversation. "He's quite upset, and as his mother I can see a good portion of that is hurt rather than anger."

Evie dropped her gaze to her lap. "I am very sorry I hurt him. I'd do anything to change that. I felt so powerless after choosing the wrong man the first time around. The ruse was meant for my protection, but not at the cost of hurting him."

"Have you told him that?" Belle asked gently.

"Yes. I begged him for his forgiveness and told him I wasn't after his wealth." She gestured around her. "As you can see, I have no need of it or a title. I simply wanted to ascertain that he was a good man with good politics. Which he is."

"Ah. You're in love with him," Eleanor said.

Although it wasn't a question, Evie answered with a glance at Belle. "Yes, and before you ask, I told him that, too."

"You did? What did he say?" Belle leaned forward.

"He laughed and said he didn't believe me and shut the door in my face." She left out that it was his bedroom door.

Xander's mother sucked in a breath.

Charlotte spoke for the first time since the inquisition had begun. "This is exactly why we're here. Your son conveniently left that part out."

Eleanor replied, "Agreed. He also left out the part that he's in love with her as well, despite the fact that 'tis fairly obvious."

Evie's mother leaned in. "Word has it he spoke to a marquess about marrying her when he thought she was a maid. Before he learned of the subterfuge."

Evie's mouth dropped. Her mother must mean Hollibrook, but he hadn't shared that tidbit with her, so how had her mother learned it? "He did what?"

"Oh?" Eleanor's face lit up. "So there is hope."

Evie shot her mother a look. They'd have words about Xander's consideration of marrying her alter ego later.

Belle was tapping her lip with a finger. "All of this makes me think his reaction was as much about the title as trust. As women, we all recognize the limitations on our choices. No one can condemn you for doing a little investigating. More than a month's worth might have been excessive, but I do understand. Perhaps more than anyone else in this room, although that is a story for another day as well."

"So what can we do?" Eleanor asked.

"We need to ensure he understands our stories, our fears. And maybe we introduce him to Penelope as well. She's an excellent example of someone trying to take their future into their own hands at a steep price. It just happened to pay off when Michael found her." Belle added to the hosts, "The Earl of Mansfield."

"Right, then. We can easily do that at our little gathering in a few days." Charlotte turned to Patience. "What is your next social event?"

When Evie's mother named the ball, Charlotte

nodded. "We will ensure Xander attends. If nothing is solved by the end of that night, we shall call again, if that is all right?"

Everyone rose and exchanged cheek kisses.

Nothing had been resolved, but Evie's heart ached a little less. It had felt like these women were on her side as much as Xander's.

And they had a plan.

Chapter Twenty-Nine

Xander stood on the Harringtons' doorstep, his mother at his side and North hovering behind him. He'd asked Luke for suggestions on gifts for the birthday earl. Luke had laughed and not been able to offer anything.

"How are you best friends?" he asked, frustrated.

"'Tis because we are best friends. The gifts I know of would not work for someone who doesn't know a good many of his secrets."

"Right, then. Cigars? Brandy?"

"Oh, I know. Latin poetry. But not Catullus or Ovid."

"You do realize I don't know any Latin. Or what he'd have read in university?"

"That's fine. Ask a bookseller. In fact, go to this one. 'Tis one we all prefer." Luke jotted down a name and address. "Even if he's read it, he'll appreciate the thought and might enjoy it again."

"Should I ask what you're getting him?"

"Nope." Luke grinned.

"Will I be an outsider in this gathering?"

"Well, some spend a bit more time together because they live in London for most of the year, but not everyone knows each other as well. 'Tis more like overlapping circles."

"I suppose I'll know enough people. Better than the ball the other night, and I muddled through that."

"That's the spirit, man!" Luke slapped him on the

back.

The day of the party was a rare semi-sunny spring day, and they were shown through the house to where Charlotte had set the gathering. A buffet table filled with pastries and finger foods stood against one wall, and additional chairs had been brought in from other rooms, making it crowded. But at the back of the room, French doors stood open to the garden, inviting guests to stand, sit, or stroll without feeling cramped.

North stopped at the buffet, giving Xander a moment to observe the occupants.

Belle and Charlotte were by the table, pointing at different things. They seemed to be arguing around mouthfuls of food, trading items from each others' plates.

Charlotte turned when they entered and gestured Eleanor over. Swallowing hastily, she created a plate for Eleanor with several delicious-looking treats and shoved it at her guest. "Please, you are the tiebreaker. Which of these is the best?"

Eleanor laughed and took a bite of one. She moaned in pleasure.

Xander made a note to try everything on that table at some point, but in the meantime, he needed to greet his host. He'd met William several times when he was here helping Luke.

The men were standing in the garden, talking, and sipping what Xander suspected was whisky except Luke's which he knew would be cider. His stepbrother hated cider and therefore would sip one slowly throughout the party to avoid his previous dependence on whisky. They introduced him to Evan Gardner, the Earl of Cheltenham, and Michael Slade, the Earl of

Mansfield. William asked if he wanted a drink and started to head inside, but Luke gestured for him to stay. "I'll get it. Enjoy your party."

As Xander followed Luke through the rear room to a library, he asked, "Are there any other people here?"

"Cheltie's and Slade's wives are here, likely in the kitchen. The other two couples who might have attended are not in London at the moment."

"Why would countesses be in the kitchen? Even I know that's unusual."

Luke snorted a laugh. "Let me ask you a different question first. Do you know my lovely bride's history?"

Xander shifted uncomfortably. "Do you mean…with your father?"

Luke smiled easily, unperturbed. "That's only a small fraction of it. You know she was a courtesan for more than a decade before I took her off the market."

Xander shook his head.

Before he could say anything, Belle slid into the crook of her husband's arm. "Nice try. I took myself off the market. You were supposed to be the last man I had to take care of."

"And so I am, love," he said, kissing her hair.

"What does this have to do with the ladies in the kitchen?" Xander asked, uncomfortable with this discussion.

"Penelope, who by the way, made all those delicious delicacies in the other room, was a working-class girl who wanted to own a bakery. She became a courtesan in order to fund that shop."

"Given the side glances I've received on the streets and in my club, with my title"—Xander's mouth twisted a little—"I confess to surprise that you are so comfortable sharing that past."

"The truth always gets out. And certainly there are invitations we'll never be privy to, but we don't want those anyway," Luke said with a shrug.

"You'd also be surprised how much is forgiven when some pompous jackass's spoiled son needs Luke's services," Belle added with a satisfied grin.

"How did Michael meet his wife?"

"Oh, he bid on her at a virgin auction, to be his courtesan," Belle replied in a blithe tone, only to laugh when Xander spewed his sip of whisky back into his glass.

Luke leaned forward, and Xander wondered if they had planned this conversation. "Cheltie met his wife when she came to him for funding to expand her apothecary business…"

Xander raised his glass, but Luke put his hand on Xander's arm to stop him from attempting another drink, "…at a sex party."

He blinked. Tried to form a response. "That's nice" didn't seem adequate. He blinked again, lowering his glass.

"Why, you might ask, are we sharing all this with you at once?" Belle asked.

Xander narrowed his eyes. He'd been correct; it *had* been preplanned. "I might."

"For two reasons." She straightened away from her husband. "First, I hope you'll understand that as a woman who worked hard to gain independence so she'd never have to rely on a man's whim for her happiness—as did Cheltie's wife, Slade's wife, possibly even your mother—I had limited ways to influence my future. Something you did not have to worry about even before you were a duke. Think about the laws you've seen and how many of them even refer to women, much less address the rights of women. We are largely ignored by society and governed at the whim of men."

Luke squeezed her shoulder, and she took a breath. "I apologize, for my fervency not my content. 'Tis a subject near and dear to my heart."

"Thank you for being so candid with me," Xander murmured. "Dare I ask what the second reason is?"

Belle smiled. "To show you that not all Londoners are nobs, not all members of the Ton value only titles, and that even a pub manager duke can be happy here when his presence is needed in Town."

Xander wondered how she'd gotten hold of that moniker. She was a formidable force, better to have as a friend than a foe.

Belle's grin turned devilish. "By the way, we went to visit Evie yesterday. And by we, I mean Charlotte, myself, and your darling mother. And Evie added one event you neglected to mention—her declaration of love and apology. She said your reaction was to laugh in her face and slam a door. I'll let you explain that one to your mother. Either way, I'd encourage you to think about the efforts other women have had to make to secure their future before deciding a well-intentioned lie is so terrible."

With that, she walked away, leaving Luke to sip his cider and wait for Xander to recover.

* * * *

Xander spent the rest of the party in near silence watching the women, the men, and the men's attendance on their women.

His mother said almost as little as he did. He wondered whether that was because she was always nervous in London or around anyone who was a lord this or lady that, or because she was waiting to talk to him about his reaction to Evie's apology. He shuddered at the prospect of that. The lesson his mother harped on the most as he and Bruce grew up was to always treat women with respect.

Luke hung close, their previous time together in London giving them more than a passing relationship. He also had deeper insight into Xander's experiences at the hands of titled lords.

North fetched his mother a plate and brought it to where she sat talking to Belle and Charlotte. His stepfather then leaned down to smooth her hair and kiss her temple, the act surprising Xander based on his experience with nobs. He'd seen them be affectionate at home, but no titled lords expressed such a thing in public.

Luke leaned in and said, "My father was never demonstrative with my mother like that. In fact, I'm not sure he was as attentive, although he loved her dearly and took years to get over her. My memories are vague, but I suspect she would have been the one making him a plate whilst he discussed politics or business."

Xander narrowed his eyes at his stepbrother. Enough was enough. They all thought there was a way back to a relationship with Evie, but he couldn't see it. "You don't need to beat me over the head with it. I got your message and Belle's. I'm not quite sure what to do with all that information, however."

"I suppose it depends on whether you're in love with her, too. The women seem to think you are, and they're rarely wrong."

Xander winced. His mother's chastisement later would include that. "I thought I was. But trust is important to me. And she broke mine in the worst way she could have—lying *and* being a titled nob."

"Did she break your trust, or hurt your feelings? If her purposes were not nefarious, then it was a mistake in judgment on her part. A terrible one, as it was, given your dislike of us 'nobs,' but a mistake. And in order to succeed, any relationship has to include forgiveness. You'll make mistakes. Hellfire, by the sound of it, you already have."

Xander pressed his lips together when Luke laughed at his own joke. "So, what? I tell her I forgive her? Then what?"

Luke guffawed, bending over as though unable to catch his breath from laughing too hard. Not the reaction he'd hoped for, and not helpful in suggesting anything better.

Belle looked around but remained sitting. Apparently, she'd said her piece.

Evan wandered over, though, and asked, "Care to share, gentlemen?"

Luke took a deep breath, opened his mouth to talk and instead began laughing again. A quick jab of Xander's elbow sobered him enough to spit out, "Xander here thinks that after laughing at Evie throwing herself on his mercy, he can just say he accepts her apology and all will be well."

When Luke said it like that, it did sound rather naïve.

Evan looked pained.

"Right, then. How did each of you manage it?" Perhaps he could learn from their approaches.

"Manage to admit that we loved our women, and we

were more wrong than they were, and we'd be forever grateful if they'd be gracious enough to allow us to serve them for the rest of our worthless lives?" Luke asked.

Evan grinned at Luke's description.

Xander nodded. That certainly sounded more attractive for a woman to hear, even if it was a bit over the top. Having struggled so hard in the past and now with his past, Xander wasn't sure he was uncomfortable with Luke's choice of the word "serve." Unbidden, the thought rose—*For Evie, I'd serve forever.*

Luke said, "You know a little of my story. After she helped me forego the evils of drink, she rejected me, not trusting me to be an equal partner, rather than a dependent. I had to prove to her I could pursue my dream in the face of adversity. When she came to me to help me mend a breach with my father and saw I didn't need her help, we were able to move forward."

Xander doubted he could handle the Ton without Evie. He'd pictured them dealing with Parliamentary decisions and alliances together, as well as balls and other social invitations. Luke's view that she'd made a mistake rather than having evil intent made sense. And while he hadn't admitted it to anyone, he had very definitely been in love with her. But he'd broken her trust as much as she'd broken his. He still wasn't sure how to fix that.

Evan sighed. "Must I?"

Luke turned to him. "Yes."

"I was, perhaps, more like you, Xander. I had the title and the wealth, and therefore Althea should be eager for me to bestow those things on her. In short, I was beyond arrogant. She refused my proposal."

Xander gaped at him and saw Luke's similar

expressions of shock. He flapped a hand. "What—How—?"

"Her cousin set me straight. Although I can see you'd all enjoy them, I'll spare myself repeating the details. I'd been so focused on overcoming my own concerns around marriage, I'd focused on my side of things. Essentially, she said I had to show Althea why it was advantageous for her and how I'd address *her* concerns, which were not my money or the title. Thankfully, the second time worked." Evan glanced over to the kitchen door where his wife was giggling with Penelope.

"No doubt it helped that you tossed in a school program and building named after her." Luke's tone was dry.

Evan grinned. "Well, yes. Never hesitate to use the tools at your disposal, young Xander."

The comment about Cheltie's building gave Xander an idea. Perhaps he did have a way to fix things with Evie. His meeting with his solicitor the next morning could not have been better timed. He turned to Evan. "My lord, might you have a spare hour tomorrow to join me at my solicitor's? I've heard you're the best investment adviser money cannot buy."

Evan grinned and agreed. "One of the two best perhaps, but I confess it's more of a hobby than anything else. I'd love to help."

* * * *

Jacob Lancaster was waiting for him the next morning when he arrived. The secretary at a desk outside Jacob's office showed him directly in through the open door where the solicitor stood to exchange bows and show him to a comfortable table.

"Tea, please, Isaac. Then we'll want the door closed."

They exchanged pleasantries while Isaac sorted the tea, Jacob inquiring as to Xander's growing comfort with his role and title.

"Your Grace, I cannot tell you how happy I am to hear all this. You seem calmer, more settled. And if I may be so bold, you've mastered so much in such a short time. The Rutland holdings are vast and varied."

"To that end, Lancaster, I'd like to review my financials with you please. Not in detail," he added when the solicitor looked alarmed. "I'd never comprehend them to that level. But I wish to gain an idea of how much of my wealth is in land, bank notes, and other investments."

"Certainly, Your Grace. Would you like to come back next week, and we will have a summary put together with some details on your largest holdings?"

"No. I'd like to do that now, Lancaster. That is why I asked you to keep your whole morning clear for me. You know it doesn't have to be pretty. There will be plenty of work to do after I see 'how the land lies' so to speak. And I should warn you that the Earl of Cheltenham will join us shortly, as I've asked him for his help."

"The Earl of…" Jacob trailed off, blinking.

"It seems you have heard of him."

The solicitor blew out a long breath, shook his hands, and wiped them on his trousers. "Yes. I hope he finds things adequate."

"Hey." Xander reached across the table and grasped the man's wrist. "You've no need to impress him. Our association will continue as long as you do right by me, and I do right by you."

Lancaster's shoulders dropped, and he gave Xander a wan smile. "Thank you, sir. Right, then. I pulled some crates out of our storage room in case you had questions. Would you mind if I asked Isaac to help us? He's a wizard with the files."

"Not at all. Can I help?"

"No, have another cup of tea, and we'll be right with you." Jacob appeared nervous but committed.

As he finished his tea, Evan arrived and introductions were made. After a half hour of digging, Jacob Lancaster and Isaac had dust on their sleeves, two crates open on Jacob's desk, and one more box pulled from storage open on the floor.

Joining Xander and Evan at the round table in the corner of the office, they sat with sighs.

"This may not be everything but it will be directionally correct." Jacob noted a list of properties, a list of bank balances, and a much shorter list of other investments.

Evan perused them, adding each column with lightning speed. He asked probing questions about the investments and whether Jacob had contemplated other ideas.

When he suggested moving some money out of banks and into steam engine pursuits, noting that he'd provide introductions, Jacob didn't lift a pen. Instead, he turned to Xander and asked, "Your Grace? Do you approve this plan?"

Evan blinked before a slow grin spread across his face. "You're a good man, Jacob Lancaster. I look forward to working with you more in the future."

Jacob turned beet red and murmured his thanks

before glancing back to Xander.

"It all sounds excellent. You both have my appreciation. Now…here is what I was wondering…"

He ran down the list of properties, pointing to several for which he'd like to give a fifty percent ownership to the man running the day-to-day business. "If my other investments can earn better returns, can I do that? And can I do something similar for my tenant farmers, without jeopardizing the wages of others in my employ or putting a future duke in a tough spot?"

Evan looked at him with interest, his brows raised. "You might have shared that goal with me yesterday, you know."

"I might have, but I needed to sleep on it to be sure."

"How much does this have to do with Evie?"

"Less than you might think."

"But some. Good. And yes, I can understand where your background might play a larger part. 'Tis an aggressive plan, but a good one. Lancaster, what think you?"

"I'd prefer to see the plan rolled out over time, as we see how the other investment returns are. However, that's my conservative approach to managing others' funds. And Lord Cheltenham here is more of an expert than I am."

Xander nodded. "If we step through it, I worry about offering some but not others, as it would appear unfair."

"You could do it property by property?" Jacob suggested.

"What about others whose employment does not allow for such a thing?" Evan asked.

Jacob dismissed that. "Servants get pensions. In fact, if anything, I'd say he's remedying an unfair balance the other way."

Evan nodded and stared at the piece of paper. "You might want to review each property and see which are more lucrative than others. Perhaps you sell some of them to simplify your life and invest that in some of the newer technologies being developed. We are becoming less and less an agrarian society."

"I can draw up those analyses and send them to you, Your Grace. You should visit some of them. Whilst not all of them are entailed, there are some beautiful homes on this list."

Xander scoffed. "I'll visit one or two, perhaps. Note which ones you'd recommend, but let's also see where they fall in terms of profits. I am overwhelmed by the size of the estate in Rutland, never mind other homes. It seems excessive."

"You might always want to consider," Evan said, his eyes twinkling, "a wife's desires, as I'm given to understand you're contemplating a marriage contract with all this."

Xander growled at him. When Jacob looked taken aback, he smoothed his face and replied, "I shall take that under advisement. Thank you, Cheltenham. Now, I have one last request, Lancaster."

Chapter Thirty

Evie was tired. Lifting a teacup was an effort and bringing a fork to her mouth more than a few times in a meal felt Herculean. She wanted to sleep, because when awake she daydreamed of Xander. Their debates about a particular bill, their playful flirting when she was working and he was supposed to be, their late night explorations in his bed.

Sleep wasn't much better, though. He overtook her dreams so when she woke tears stained her cheeks.

Her thoughts circled with wild ideas to beg his forgiveness again. Tempted to offer him a year more of maid service, she imagined the sexy mischief they could get up to in his library every day. However, part of her sorrow was that he couldn't see her good intentions. He'd had more respect for her as a maid than he did for her as a lady. Yet she was indeed a lady.

Her goal all along was to see if he would be a suitable husband. Now she knew—she wanted that marriage contract if he could show Lady Evelyn the respect he'd shown the mob-capped Evie.

She'd even live without love. Love had never been something she'd aspired to in a marriage, and she needn't start now. Having someone who shared her life views and would raise their children with similar beliefs was the most important thing.

Mmm…children. We'll need lots of practice to

ensure he has heirs. Sighing at her wayward thoughts, Evie punched the pillow and rolled over on the chaise longue, nearly falling off. She did not care that it was the middle of the afternoon and she was supposed to be visiting or sewing or doing some charitable deed. She was tired.

Her mother bustled into her room followed by her maid. "Let's see what she— Evie, are you all right, child?"

Mama perched on the edge of the chaise with a hand to Evie's forehead.

"Mama, I'm not sick. Just tired." Too late, she wondered if she should have pleaded a health issue. Was that other ball her parents had been discussing tonight or tomorrow?

"Oh good. Rest for another hour. But after that you must rise and ready yourself for the ball."

"Can you not go without me? Just to this one. Please, Mama."

"No, I won't hear of it. You need to be there. If the Duke of Rutland dissolves the betrothal, everyone needs to see 'twas his fault not yours, that you are not lacking in any way."

"Mama, if the Duke of Rutland dissolves the betrothal, I don't care if anyone else thinks I'm lacking. Only his opinion counts."

"Hush. You cannot think like that. If he doesn't want you, then *he* is lacking. You deserve better than a man who cannot forgive. It means that there's a better choice out there for you."

Evie whined, "But I don't want a better choice. I want him." She was being dramatic but couldn't help how she felt. Society had grown tiresome. Xander had taught her there were more important things in life.

"Well, what if he attends tonight? He's in Town, and I have it on good authority that he's been invited."

Evie blinked, then sat up. "Do I have time for a bath?"

Her mother turned to the maid to order a bath, not realizing Evie could see her satisfied smirk in the mirror over her dresser.

She didn't care if her mother was manipulating her. The temptation of being in his presence once more was too much to resist. Aunt Lou had said that the best way to win him back was in person.

Besides, she'd avoided him at the previous event, so this might be the last time her eyes could feast on him. Perhaps she could finagle introducing him to more Whigs. If only she could do that on his arm as his betrothed. Or else she'd watch him from a balcony and pine silently. She'd take what she could get, despite knowing it would drive a stake through her heart all over again.

* * * *

Despite having fewer attendees, the ball was a crush due to the host's home being smaller. Sitting in the line of coaches spewing partygoers one by one, she snickered thinking what Xander would say about such a fête. Likely it would be something about whether the host attempted to navigate the overheated, smelly ballroom to actually speak to all of his guests.

Unsure what she'd do if he attended, she also worried whether he'd ignore her. Her mother would become apoplectic if she perceived a public snub, but Evie was more concerned that such an action would indicate a permanent severing of their relationship. She needed that last shard of hope to cling to.

After being handed out of the carriage by her father, they entered and made their way to the ballroom. As they stood in the doorway, Xander's close-cropped head drew her gaze like a beacon.

The announcement of their names was lost in the melee, yet he whipped around and stared. His lips moved, making his excuses, because in the next moment he was striding through the crowd toward her, parting them as easily if they were blades of grass.

Reaching her and her parents, he bowed in turn and asked, "Evie, might I have a word?"

Her brows twitched, and she looked around them. "Here? Now?"

"Er, sort of."

"Go take a stroll around the ballroom, my dear," her mother encouraged, ignoring the fact that two people could not promenade through the crowd.

Her father shot both of them a warning look but said nothing. Instead, he raised a hand to someone over Xander's shoulder and murmured to his wife to excuse him.

Xander proffered his arm, and Evie placed her hand on it, hoping he had a plan. She smothered a grin when he angled his outer shoulder in front of them and led her through the crowd toward the French doors that opened to a veranda. Here was yet another reason to appreciate this man's physique.

As he stepped through them, Evie balked, not wanting to risk her reputation if he was going to end things between them. She planted her feet, tugged on his sleeve, and whispered, "What do you want with me,

Xander? If you still plan to break the betrothal, the last thing you want is to be caught alone with me."

"I understand, Evie. If you're more comfortable, we can stay here at the railing, in sight of the ballroom. There are others out here, serving as chaperone."

Her nerves had come to the forefront, however, and she couldn't wait any longer. "Just tell me what you want, please."

"I want...," he swallowed and took a breath. "To accept your apology and offer one of my own."

Her brows climbed her forehead. This was unexpected—pleasantly so, but she was unprepared. She stared at him, speechless and expectant. If he thought those words were enough, he was sorely mistaken.

Turning to face her, he took her hands in his. "I was hurt. My feelings, my pride, all of it. I had bared my soul to you, and suddenly, you were a stranger. Worse, a titled stranger. So I lashed out rather than listen to what you were telling me."

He appeared contrite, his eyes pleading and his brows drawn up. But she still hadn't heard a clear apology, just reasons. He might have reasons again in a week, a month, a year, and who knows what he'd do then. She stared at him, remaining silent.

He glanced down at their joined hands, then up again. Sighed. Shifted.

He might be nervous, but she needed more.

"I did not comprehend your situation. Nor, I confess, did I attempt to. My family and friends here have helped me gain that understanding. Apparently, Luke's wife is not the only one who was previously a courtesan."

Evie blinked twice. Had he just compared her to a courtesan? She took a breath to speak.

"Blazes." Xander's eyes were wide. At least he seemed to recognize his faux pas. "Ah, I refer to that to demonstrate my new appreciation for the lengths women have to go to pursue some level of autonomy in this world."

"Right." She narrowed her eyes. "That covers your acceptance of *my* apology."

"Yes…"

"I've yet to hear yours, though." She raised her brows.

"Right, right. I was getting there." He shuffled his feet again. "I know 'tis presumptuous of me after my reaction, but I ask for your empathy regarding my reaction. I had told you my experiences with titled nobs. That colored my reaction to your, er, error in judgment in waiting so long to tell me who you were."

Her thoughts raced as Xander spun out his apology. It was a decent apology, as they went. However, there was no guarantee he'd truly learned from it. Would he be mean and run away and only come back if friends set him straight in the future?

She supposed that even if he'd said he'd learned his lesson, one never knew until the next time. At least he was here, talking to her. And he couldn't run off quite so easily if they were married.

She almost chuckled when he'd called her lie of omission an error in judgment. She owed his friends—or more likely their wives—a debt of gratitude for that reshaping. But the subject was too serious to let it go with a laugh at a phrase.

When he wound down, she realized she'd been waiting for a declaration of love, mirroring hers. It was obvious he cared for her and that he was a caretaker of everyone around him. And it wasn't fair to expect him to feel the same; she'd simply hoped.

Trying to formulate a reply, she squeezed his hands.

He squeezed back and began speaking again. "I visited with my solicitor. The Earl of Cheltenham helped—"

Evie gasped, distracted by that tidbit. "You know the Earl of Cheltenham well enough to get favors from him? How did you manage that?"

"You've heard of him? His reputation is more illustrious than I realized." He squinted for a moment. "As I remember it, Luke's wife is best friends with one of his closest friends. Anyway, he helped rearrange my finances. You should know that I'm giving half ownership of a large portion of my properties to the people who run them. And I may sell a few of the country homes."

She was agog. This was caretaking to a whole new level. "Xander, I assume if Lord Cheltenham looked at your investments, you can do this without harm to your own standard of living and those in your employ. This is amazing. Beyond amazing. And generous. And-and I can't think of adjectives right now, I'm so surprised."

"You're not concerned? Or...angry?" He peered at her as though trying to read her sincerity in the dim lighting of the veranda.

"Why on earth would I be angry?"

"If you accept the marriage contract with me, it would affect you."

Oh. What a lovely thought. He was going to need to do better than that, though. She wasn't going through all this again when he had a snit and decided to reject it. She raised a brow. "I understood that you'd declined it."

He clutched her hands, and she swore he might be sweating.

She stared at him, willing him to say what she needed to hear. The whole party might have joined them on the veranda for all she knew. Xander filled her vision. Her heart beat double time in hope.

His voice tremulous, he begged, something she would never have expected the proud pub manager to do. "Please, please accept my apology? Life without you is miserable. I miss my companion in the library so much, my partner in debating the merits of bills and making financial decisions. Cheltie be damned. I am in love with you, and I wish to marry you as quickly as your parents will allow. Please, Lady Evelyn, become the Duchess of Rutland so you can continue to teach me how to be a dratted duke?"

Tears formed and her shoulders dropped in relief as he said all the things she'd been waiting for. A sob escaped her, and she bit her lip.

He loved her!

"Are you sure? You won't run off again if I make a mistake? And you'll come to London occasionally to see my family?" She could actually live without the last one, as they'd proven they'd travel to her, but she threw it out there to test how far he'd go for her.

"Yes. Absolutely yes to all of it. Anything you want if you'll have me. And you have final say before I— we—sell any properties. We can take a wedding trip to visit all of them."

She laughed through her tears at his eagerness. Everything she'd ever hoped for was on offer, and she couldn't wait another minute to accept. "Then, yes, I wish to be your wife, title or no. I've missed Mrs. Betters and Duncan and the house, too."

He gathered her into his arms, but at her last statement leaned back and asked, "You're not marrying me for them, are you?"

She patted his shoulder. "No, you dolt. I told you I loved you ages ago. I was waiting for you to catch up."

He laughed and leaned down as though to kiss her.

She in turn leaned back. "Xander, be sure. We're at a ball. Kissing is beyond scandalous. Even this embrace is enough to compromise me."

"I'm sorry." He stepped back.

"No, no, don't run away again. I don't care in the least. But I want you to be very sure before my father is told we are out here."

He leaned in and kissed her. "As I said, your wish is my command, my lady. Yours is the only opinion I care about."

As they turned to go inside, the Earl of Craven was indeed at the doors watching, but not interfering, standing next to North.

Xander sketched a shallow bow and asked, "Sir, may I call on you tomorrow to finalize the particulars of the betrothal? I'd like to claim my bride as soon as possible."

Her father looked at her and waited for her nod before responding, "I look forward to it."

Chapter Thirty-One

The contract had been modified for his name, the bans had been posted, and in what felt like no time at all, Xander found himself dressing for his wedding. He'd spent every minute he could with Evie, and every other minute either planning their tour of their properties or doing almost anything to avoid dealing with the logistics of the wedding day itself.

Bruce had made it down from Northumberland, as had Evie's Aunt Louisa from Rutland. They'd kept the invitations to the ceremony and the breakfast following it to a minimum.

Evie's father had a few cronies who had been like uncles to her. The Marquess of Hollibrook had been invited, but sent his regrets with his well wishes. And they both agreed that Xander's new friends should be there. The women at least had been rooting for this union, and he hoped they would become fast friends with Evie.

Despite Bruce and Luke both keeping him company last night and this morning at North's London home, and the brevity of the guest list, Xander was becoming increasingly anxious.

What if someone took issue with Bruce's presence? Or for that matter, Belle's? It wouldn't do for a duke to engage in fisticuffs at his own wedding. Given his anxiety, if someone said something even slightly derogatory, that outcome would become more and more likely. He did not want to embarrass Evie or upset her or her family in any way.

His mother and North met them downstairs in the front hallway. When Xander yanked at his cravat twice on the way down the stairs, North stepped aside and spoke to the footman.

As the five of them climbed into the carriage, Frazer came hurrying out and joined the coachman on the driver's seat.

Alighting at the church, Xander yanked at his tie once again. He strode into the building, intent on finding Evie and getting this done. Why hadn't they hied off to Gretna Green, dammit? He wanted to marry her more than anything, but the formality of this even more than balls was unnerving.

The others hurried after him.

His mother caught his arm and said, "I see Cravens' carriage on the street. Allow Frazer to fix your cravat and then keep your hands off it for a quarter hour, please."

"Yes, Mama." He modified his internal dialogue. He didn't want to embarrass Evie or his mother. Taking a deep breath, he focused on the fact that he was marrying the love of his life. Once Evie's hand was in his, even before the words were spoken linking them forever, he'd relax.

His mother put her palms on his cheeks, then dropped one hand to hold his and reached for Bruce's with her other. "I am so proud of both of you. You are both good men, and I am glad Xander has found a lovely woman who recognizes that. I am so happy."

With that she burst into tears. As the brothers rolled their eyes and patted her shoulders, North hurried over.

He steered her away and folded her into a hug, freeing Xander to Frazer's ministrations.

They paced down the center aisle, nodding to guests already in attendance. The organ began, and all fidgets and feelings of strangulation flew out of his head, because there was his bride. The first thing he noticed was her gleaming chestnut hair. No more scratchy caps for her, and although jeweled combs kept it away from her face, his fingers itched to run through the rest of it. She was in a copper gown, the folds of the skirt catching the light and shining as though they were truly metal. He smirked. The color both mocked and elevated the idea of a brown maid's uniform, and the grin lurking on her lips told him it had been a deliberate choice. Only his Evie would think of such an idea. Her lips were a warm rose against her pale face, and he guessed he might not be alone in his nerves. He clasped her hand in his as she reached him and gave it a quick kiss, ignoring her mother's gasp. The clergyman had to clear his throat twice to get Xander's attention off his bride.

After the ceremony, he could not say what transpired. He would never be able to recall his full formal address that included several lesser titles. Thankfully, Jacob Lancaster had been happy to provide those to the minister presiding over the ceremony.

At last, he and Evie were in the carriage. Alone. Only then did he release her hand to cradle her head and angle his mouth across hers. Sweet peace swept over him. She was his. He was hers. Forever.

There was still the wedding breakfast to get through, and he was still uncomfortable with the various titles, names, and nicknames. It seemed most of the men had at least one nickname, sometimes more. He'd learned some on his previous stay with Luke and Belle—Luke was South, or Lyon, or Lynwood, as well as Luke. It was exhausting, trying to recall how to introduce people to others. Once inside, he again clutched Evie's hand on his arm with his other hand and refused to let go, declining food or drink.

They would be at his London home for the night before departing for two of his homes in the south to evaluate them for sale. North and his mother had hosted the breakfast thankfully, so he hoped to escape this purgatory soon.

When Evie asked for a private moment, he sighed in relief and nodded. When they stepped into the rear drawing room, his parents were waiting.

Evie turned and said, "I already said my goodbyes to my parents. It's been clear you are not enjoying yourself, so say farewell, and I will have the carriage brought around."

With that, she kissed the older couple on the cheek, thanking them each in turn, and hurried out. He turned.

"It does not seem fair to skip out on guests who are as much ours as yours."

"'Tis your wedding day. The bride and groom are exempt from fairness, and almost everyone in there has been anxious to start their wedding night at one point," North said, with a smile at Eleanor who was tucked under his arm.

"Eh, now I feel a little sick, and I haven't even eaten anything," Xander replied with a grin.

"Oh, away with you. You enjoy your night and we'll enjoy ours. So there," his mother teased.

Grimacing, he kissed her cheek before hugging North. "I owe you both a huge debt of gratitude. You helped me when this mess began, you helped me navigate London, and more importantly, you supported my quest to win back Evie. We shall send you a card from our travels and come see you soon."

In the front hall, Evie was nowhere to be seen, but the footman directed him outside and pointed to the carriage with the closed curtains. Inside, Evie was waiting for him, a smile on her face. He returned it, relishing the knowledge that he'd won the rights to all of her smiles. He grabbed the cravat pin he'd made note of that morning and removed it, tossing it in her lap to yank at his neckcloth.

She chuckled as he slid it free and leaned in to place a gentle finger in the hollow of his throat, murmuring, "Mine."

When he reached for her to drag her into a tight hug, it might have held the remnants of relief, but as that drained away, happiness filled him as her scent encircled him.

* * * *

In his bedroom, another fantastically comfortable bed beckoned. Xander stared at it. He had every intention of that being their marital bed for every night. Evie could do what she wanted with the duchess's suite.

The best way to make her want that, too, would be to make this night perfect for her. He grew nervous. Excited, certainly, but also apprehensive. He'd waited so long for this moment, as had she, and he wanted it so badly he wasn't sure he could be patient.

For a moment, he wished they'd engaged in the fullest of intimacies in Rutland, where there were no expectations, just two people in love. But he couldn't regret any of their trials and tribulations, as it had brought them to this moment.

He spoke his thought out loud. "You're mine forever, now, my little maid."

"And you're mine, my pub manager cum duke."

That sounded spectacular. Gulping a breath in, he spun her and found the fastenings of her dress. Pausing to palm his erection and remind himself to keep things slow, he undid them one at a time.

She shivered under his touch. "Xander, hurry, please."

"We have all night, love." But it was gratifying to hear that she might be as impatient as he was.

"Yes, but you've kept me waiting for weeks!" she exclaimed.

He laughed under his breath, but when she turned around and he saw the stunning corset and embroidered chemise under it, barely covering the rose-hued tips of her breasts, his laughter caught in his throat.

"Evie." He batted her hands away as she reached for his waistcoat, needing to cement this picture in his memory. "Let me look at you. I always pictured you like this. In silk and satin, because that is what you deserve. I hated seeing you in that maid's uniform. And I spent more time thinking about your gorgeous hair hidden under that cap than I did about my correspondence. You are every inch a lady and were always going to be *my* lady, uniform and cap or not."

"Husband, you've forever ruined my appreciation for a well-tied cravat or a sparkly cravat pin. I never knew how sexy a man's throat could be. Your throat, anyway. But now, I need to see more of you." With that she pushed his chest.

Xander allowed himself to be pressed onto the edge of the bed. Evie dragged his waistcoat off, made short work of his shirt, then attacked the fall of his trousers.

Unable to remove the rest of his clothes with him sitting, she tugged at him again. Instead, he took matters into his own hands to hasten the process, leaning down to remove his shoes before standing and shucking the trousers, stockings, and smallclothes. He spread his arms wide and smiled at his wife. "There. Is that better?"

"Oh, yes." Her whispered words were a stark contrast to the shove that sent him back onto the bed, half lying with his feet still on the floor. "Now, where to start…"

Still in her petticoats, chemise, and corset, she clambered on him, settling across his thighs. There, she paused, looking flummoxed.

He chuckled, enjoying the view but ready to move things along. "I appreciate your eagerness, my lovely bride. But perhaps if you allowed me to lead this once? You can have a turn later."

She nodded, chagrined.

Chapter Thirty-Two

Evie was so eager to experience total intimacy with Xander, she literally did not know what to do first, second, or third. They had been chaperoned closely these past few weeks, with very little alone time allowed. When they stole a few private moments together, Xander refused to complete the act, stating that she deserved better than a quick tupping over his desk. Several rather inventive curse words had crossed her lips that day, but he only laughed and tossed out a new parliamentary bill, saying that it would kill any desire she may have had.

She'd been so focused on getting him naked, she hadn't taken the time to remove the articles of clothing she still wore, and now she was stumped. His entire body lay out before her like a buffet of sweets, only she couldn't decide what she wanted to sample first. Their bedroom activities had always been Xander teaching her, so she schooled herself to patience and allowed him to take over.

As he slid her off him, she dragged her nails over his nipples and down his chest, eliciting a groan.

"Minx," he said.

She shrugged a shoulder with a half grin. There was no reason she couldn't play even when overwhelmed.

He stood to make fast work of the remaining pieces she wore, setting down the exquisite beribboned corset with care onto a nearby chaise, giving her the enticing scenery of his naked muscles moving in the afternoon light from the window. This beautiful kind man was now her husband, partner, and equal. She was still coming to terms with the degree of happiness that brought her, although she might never fully understand it.

Swooping her up, he cradled her in his arms and kissed her. Longing replaced her overwhelm as she kissed him back, trying to get closer and closer to him. He laid her on the bed, staring at her as she had at him. The air that now separated them created goosebumps all over her skin, making her shiver.

Their love lay between them in every look, kiss, and caress. When his mouth met hers, he showed his respect for her thoughts and words. His lips on her breast reminded her that their hearts were one now. And his worship of her most delicate flesh with his lips and tongue and fingers reinforced their future, a lifetime to explore one another.

Every stroke felt new, every kiss had a greater meaning, as though they repeated their vows with each new touch.

Sensation and emotion twined together, spreading like fast-growing vines through her body, right to her fingertips. She undulated beneath him, craving more. His fingers fluttered through the curls over her most sensitive flesh, but did not allow her to seek a firmer touch, holding her still with his upper body leaning over her. She could not stop kissing him to beg anyway.

Finally, she stopped clutching him and shoved, catching him unawares.

He fell back, and she climbed over him once again, mimicking his actions in a procession down his body.

Before she got far, one hand on his cock and her lips

on his nipple, his hand slipped between her legs and thrummed her swollen, needy nub. She shuddered and lost focus on what she'd been doing.

He took advantage and flipped her again, nestling his hips between hers as he rumbled, "I need you."

Beyond words, she nodded, widening her legs to welcome him.

He notched his cock at her entrance and slid home, making Evie gasp. There was a twinge of pain; he was large and she tight. But after that, nothing had ever felt quite so right to her. It was the strangest combination of comfortable and thoroughly exciting, as though she'd been made for this man and he for her.

Nothing would ever separate them again.

He moved as though to withdraw, and she gasped again and clutched him to her. *No!*

But oh lud, he surged back in and there was a new level of sensation, like another layer of cake, building on the last one.

"All right?" he grunted.

This was beyond anything she could have imagined, even after experiencing his fingers and tongue. The bond, the fullness of having part of him inside her while they were face to face, wove the physical and emotional response together, the frosting on the cake of rising bliss. "My word, Xander. Do that again, please."

He laughed at her polite request and complied, over and over again.

Soon she was rising to meet him and clawing at his back to get him to move faster.

He leaned up, changing the angle of his cock inside her and hit a new spot that made every muscle in her body clench.

Two thrusts later, her orgasm exploded, cascading over her, tightening then loosening all the muscles that had clenched as she shuddered with pleasure. "Xander!"

His cock bucked inside her as her channel rippled around him, and he stiffened, stilling as he groaned his ecstasy.

He nuzzled her ear for a minute while he caught his breath and collapsed to the bed in a roll, ending on his back with her tucked into his side.

"Worth the wait?" he asked.

"Yes, but I still wish we'd been doing that for the past month."

"Oh, there is much more to learn, never fear." She snuggled her bottom against him and closed her eyes with a smile lingering on her lips.

Epilogue

Their wedding trip had been full of fun and laughter, in between sexual romps in various rooms in assorted homes belonging to the dukedom, and even the carriage once.

Evie was so happy to be back in Rutland, she squealed and hugged every servant. They had lined up to formally greet the duke's bride and had applauded when she stepped out of the carriage. As she hugged each one, they followed her down the line until she was surrounded.

Xander stood on the second step and mock pouted. "I never got this sort of greeting. She's my bride, not yours."

They all ignored him until she'd checked in with every servant to see how they were doing.

Mrs. Betters whipped Evie's mob cap from behind her back and offered it to the new duchess. "What shall I do with this?"

Xander snorted.

Evie said, "Burn it. Those are most uncomfortable; however do you all wear them?"

"Oh no." He stepped forward and snatched it, tucking it into his waistcoat, where his cravat already lived, bulging the pocket. "I want that for posterity, thank you."

She looked at him doubtfully, and he winked at her. *Oh*. She could see role play in their future, one late night in the library. She hoped her drab brown dress was still about somewhere.

Xander had warned her he was going to excuse himself and venture on to the pub before the horses were put up, so she was unsurprised when his voice rumbled, "Why don't you all have tea in the kitchen and everyone can share their adventures?"

The servants were only a little surprised given his familiarity with them to date, and Evie started inside, calling, "Yes, please."

Two hours later, she heard the carriage on the drive. She'd requested a cold platter of meat pie, cheese, and bread in the library, and sent everyone to bed early.

Dressed in only the mob cap and her bridal chemise, she knelt on a cushion near his desk to await him. She'd had the candles dimmed in the hall and left the door open so light from the open library door would direct him to her.

He was whistling under his breath as he entered. The song cut off mid-breath as he stumbled to a halt to stare at her. Banks, the pub manager—no, owner now—likely had plied him with ale.

Perhaps tipsy Xander would be as much fun as sober Xander. Pushing to find out, she asked, "How may I serve you, Your Grace?"

A grin spread across his face, and he drawled, "Well, if it isn't my favorite downstairs maid. Ah, but what are you doing here so late at night? It seems you might be up to mischief."

"No trouble, sir. I wasn't certain my duties were finished for the day. In fact—" She crawled under his desk, making it a point to shake her bottom. "—I think this area could use some dusting."

"I can think of something that could use some polishing, little maid." But he hadn't moved.

"Can I reach it from under here?" Tipsy Xander apparently needed things spelled out for him, she thought with a giggle.

He sat in his chair with a thud and scooted it forward a bit. Then shoved it back to undo the falls of his trousers before sliding his hips forward and slouching. Taking his cock out, he demanded, "Polish this knob, little maid."

His guffaw of laughter made her roll her eyes, thankfully where he couldn't see her, still under his desk. But she knew how to redirect his focus. He'd been teaching her more and more sexual positions and techniques throughout their wedding trip.

She leaned in, licked it from root to tip, and slid her mouth over it until her lips hit his hand at the base.

"Evie," he groaned, reaching for her head. Encountering the cap, he tugged it off and sank his fingers into her hair.

She moaned around his cock and glided her mouth up and down faster.

"We may have to re-enact this fantasy again soon. Right now, I need you up and bent over my desk. I've spent far too many nights imagining spearing into you over the papers we'd discussed that day, making you writhe on my cock."

Heat spread through her at the images his words provoked. As he shoved the chair back farther, she scrambled to obey.

She whipped the chemise off, letting it float to the desk where he'd tossed her mob cap. His hand pushed between her shoulders, leading her down.

"Grab the other side of the desk. This might be fast."

His voice above her was rough with need.

No sooner had she gripped the wood than he was sliding into her in one sharp, deep motion. Her moan was overlaid by his.

His hips began a rhythm, a slow withdrawal to almost the tip followed by a fast thrust burying himself inside her.

Her nipples chafed back and forth along the blotter, creating their own friction, and on those inward drives, his bollocks slapped that tiny bundle of nerves that sped her closer to orgasm.

He bent his knees a degree, and his cockhead rubbed that spot along the front wall of her channel that made her clench. "Yes, Xander, please, just like that."

Three more repetitions took her all the way over, and she twisted on the desk, rubbing the tips of her breasts as her inner muscles spasmed in ecstasy.

Xander pounded into her twice more, yelling, "I love you, wife."

And she responded in kind. "I love you, Your Grace."

* * *

Want to read about Charlotte and William, Luke and Belle, and other characters?

The **School of Enlightenment** Series includes:

Roslynn's Rebellion
(free prequel with newsletter signup)
He wants to bury his secrets. She is creating a new secret school. Can they work together?

Sophia's Schooling
An innocent country girl...a jaded earl...an education in pleasure.

Penelope's Passion
Schooled in the art of pleasure, her real passion is baking. Required to marry, the earl's heir finds his new courtesan more to his taste.

Althea's Awakening
A widow with no knowledge of carnal desire, a rake bored with even the most hedonistic pleasures, and a game of truth or dare…

Beth's Behavior
An outrageous free spirit meets her match in an introvert with a secret leather business.

Helen's House
Even at an all-girls school in Regency England, workplace romances can prove challenging.

Ann's Angel
(*Christmas short story*)
Two courtesans looking to get out of the game…

The **Control Series** includes:

Charlotte's Control
A young rake soon to inherit an impoverished estate…a lonely widow unable to produce an heir…a love they must forsake

<u>Lyon's Lover</u>
Under Isabella's reluctant tutelage, Luke must come to
terms with his lack of self-control and face his father,
which might just take a Christmas miracle.

Folly's Folly
Coming 2026

About the Author

Maggie Sims began her love affair with romance before her teen years, drawn to the Regency by her mum's British influence. In her twenties, she did her best to live the Carrie Bradshaw life in New York City, albeit with less expensive shoes and more books.

Despite reading hundreds of romance novels in her life, she was still blown away when she met the love of her life, an ex-Marine cinnamon roll with creative woodworking and culinary skills.

Having retired from corporate life, they live in Central Texas and are parents to a varying number of dogs and cats. When not writing, Maggie is a wine enthusiast, a travel junkie, and a romance reading fiend. She also sporadically crochets for KnotsofLove.org and does just enough exercise for that second glass of wine at night.

To find out more about Maggie's latest reads, favorite wines, and travel destinations, sign up for her newsletter.

~*~

Contact Maggie at
www.MaggieSims.com

www.ingramcontent.com/pod-product-compliance
Lightning Source LLC
Chambersburg PA
CBHW060405310726
48976CB00003B/943

9798890444073